Lauren Layne is the *New York Times* bestselling author
of more than two dozen romantic comedies.

Her books have sold over a million copies, in eight languages. Lauren's
work has been featured in *Publishers Weekly*, *Glamour*, *The Wall
Street Journal* and *Inside Edition*. She is based in New York City.

Join Lauren at **www.laurenlayne.com**
to get news on her latest books.

Just some of the reasons to indulge yourself in Lauren Layne's irresistible romances:

'Chic and clever! *Passion on Park Avenue* comes to
life like a sexy, comedic movie on the page'
Tessa Bailey, *New York Times* bestselling author

'A charming, witty, and lively narrative that reads
like a '90s rom-com' *BookBub*

'I couldn't put it down! . . . I love a sassy heroine
and a funny hero and Layne delivers both . . . Lauren Layne
knocks this one right out of Park Avenue!'
Samantha Young, *New York Times* bestselling author

'Featuring wine in coffee mugs, dinner parties with ulterior
motives, and Naomi and Oliver being (almost) caught with
their pants down, this is perfect for readers who love the
dishy women's fiction of Candace Bushnell' *Booklist*

'Layne is one of the best authors writing today and I was
reminded of that as I read this book . . . It was hot and sexy
and sweet. I laughed and shrieked and cried, exactly what
I want from a book' *Obsessed with Romance*

'[A] breezy and satisfying contemporary romance . . .
Sparkling dialogue, hilarious wedding planning scenes,
and deeply emotional moments see the series end
on a high note' *Publishers Weekly*

'A   two
be   way'

By Lauren Layne

LAUREN LAYNE

HEADLINE
ETERNAL

The right of Lauren Layne to be identified as the Author of
the Work has been asserted by her in accordance with the
Copyright, Designs and Patents Act 1988.

Published by arrangement with Gallery Books,
An Imprint of Simon & Schuster, Inc.

First published in Great Britain in 2021
by HEADLINE ETERNAL
An imprint of HEADLINE PUBLISHING GROUP

1

Cataloguing in Publication Data is available from the British Library

ISBN 978 1 4722 7532 5

Offset in 10.45/15.915 pt Janson Text LT Std by Jouve (UK), Milton Keynes

Printed and bound in Great Britain by Clays Ltd, Elcograf S.p.A.

Headline's policy is to use papers that are natural, renewable and recyclable
products and made from wood grown in sustainable forests. The logging
and manufacturing processes are expected to conform to the
environmental regulations of the country of origin.

HEADLINE PUBLISHING GROUP
An Hachette UK Company
Carmelite House
50 Victoria Embankment
London EC4Y 0DZ

www.headlineeternal.com
www.headline.co.uk
www.hachette.co.uk

To Sir, With Love

My dear Lady,

I'm not sure how to say this politely, so I'll just say it. You're incorrect in every sense of the word. You haven't lived until you've tried a lemon sorbet on a hot summer day in the city. Ice cream, by comparison, is so very pedestrian. I thought I knew you.

Yours in gentle contempt,

Sir

————————

To Sir, with equal contempt, less gentle:

I stand by my assertion that sorbet is an affront to frozen treats everywhere. I'll see your lemon sorbet and raise you a pistachio gelato any day of the year.

Lady

One

"What am I looking at here? What is that smile?"

I drop my cell phone back into my bag and turn my full attention to the baby settled on my thighs, my hand resting protectively over his warm tummy. I wipe a tiny bit of drool from his adorable mouth. "That smile is me plotting to steal this baby. And maybe the baby's beautiful daddy."

My best friend is unfazed by my threats to steal her child and husband. "Never going to work. Felix assures me he's partial to Jewish women. Oh, and he likes big boobs."

"I can convert." I make a cooing noise at the baby. "And get a boob job."

"I hope those fake boobs produce milk. Because Matteo here's still breastfeeding."

"You're a boob man already, hmm?" I ask the baby, who wraps tiny fingers around my own and shakes, grinning at me.

"Not for long," Rachel says. "I'm trying to wean the little bastard, but bottles make this one gassy."

"Farts from bottles?" I look over. "That's a thing?"

"Oh, trust me," Rachel says in a dark tone. "It's a thing. Too bad there's not a return or exchange policy for children."

"No need." I make smooching noises at the baby. "I'm stealing him, remember?"

"So you said in your attempt to distract me, but back to your Disney princess smile over whatever you were looking at on your phone. I've known you for over twenty years, and I *know* that smile. You're in your Cinderella mode."

"I do not have a Cinderella mode."

"You totally do," Rachel says. "I just watched you feed half your sandwich to the pigeons. Who you *named*."

"Are you even a real New Yorker if you don't befriend pigeons in Central Park?"

"And then you sang to them," Rachel continues.

"I hummed. A slight but crucial distinction."

"Mmm-hmm, and what song did you *hum*?"

I purse my lips and refrain from answering the question. I'd been humming "It Had to Be You," Frank Sinatra style. To the pigeons. Which, when not in my so-called Cinderella mode, I know are basically sky-rats.

This isn't looking good for me, and we both know it.

Rachel very slowly shakes her head. "Gracie Madeleine Cooper, you are in *love* and you didn't tell me."

I snort. "That'd be a hell of a feat, considering I haven't been on a second date in almost six months and *waaaaay* too many first ones."

She holds out her palm. "Phone."

"What?"

"That dreamy smile comes on your face every time you check your phone." She reaches over me to grab my purse in the confident, overbearing way of a best friend of twenty years. "Let me see it."

"What? No! Here," I say, trying to maneuver Matteo into her arms. "Let's trade. Your baby for my privacy."

Her jaw drops. "You *never* want privacy! You have a secret!"

"I do not have a secret!"

I do. I *totally* have a secret, and it's delicious and also a tiny bit embarrassing to admit, even to someone who's held my hair back over the toilet of a Coney Island bathroom after too much blue cotton candy.

I manage to safely get the baby back into her arms, and Matteo takes my side and starts to fuss, granting me a brief reprieve from my best friend's prying. As though reading my mind about the hair thing, Rachel shifts Matteo to her shoulder and hands me a hair band. "Tail me," she orders, turning her back to me.

Obediently, I gather her thick hair and attempt to wind the elastic around her mass of gorgeous curls. I smile as a childhood memory bubbles up. Me, on the first day of third grade at a new school, my ponytail a lumpy mess, courtesy of my widowed father who did his best but didn't know the first thing about little girls' hair.

Rachel, the definitive alpha of Jefferson Elementary's third-grade class, had taken one look at my stricken face, marched over, and announced that she needed to practice her French braiding and that I was her muse.

We've been styling each other's hair ever since.

"You have the best hair," I say, tucking an errant curl into the band and studying my handiwork.

"Attempt to distract from the matter at hand rejected," she says, turning back around.

"You're such a weirdo." But I sigh and relent. "Okay, if I tell you what's going on, you have to promise not to lecture."

She makes a mock-wounded face. "If you care about me at all, you wouldn't ask me to deny my true nature."

"Fine," I relent. "But *as* you lecture, at least try to remember that I already have an older sister who has yet to grasp that I'm thirty-three and not ten."

"I will take it into consideration. Proceed."

I take my time, leaning back on the green park bench, studying the cheerful energy of Central Park at lunchtime on a late summer's day.

I exhale. "So there's this dating app."

"Tinder?"

"No."

"Hinge?"

"No."

"eHarmony?"

"Okay, you rattled those off way too quickly for someone who's been married for seven years," I say. "And it's called MysteryMate."

Rachel makes a face. "Oh, I don't like the sound of this at all. There is no good use for the word *mate* outside of the Discovery Channel."

"Yeah, the name's not great," I say.

Their tagline's even worse: *Love at no sight*. And that's not even the embarrassing part of my secret.

"So how does it work?" she asks.

I reach over and rip off a piece of her unfinished sandwich and toss it to my pigeon friends, Spencer and Katharine, as in Tracy and Hepburn.

"So, you know how Tinder is all about first impressions based on someone's photo?" I say. "Well, this is sort of the opposite. There are no photos. No names, even. Instead you choose from these little cartoon avatar things and a screen name, and the app matches you with potential *mates*."

I emphasize the word deliberately with a grin, and she rolls her eyes. "Okay, I get it. The app is all 'beauty is on the *inside*.' What happens after you're matched?"

I shrug. "You message each other. If you click, you set up a meeting in person."

"But what if the other person's *hideous*?"

I give her a gently chiding look, and she shrugs as she rubs the baby's back. "It's a fair question. A meeting of the minds is nice, but physical attraction is *hot*."

"Well, so far, none of the guys I've decided to meet in person have been *hideous*."

"But one of them *was* hot, huh? Oh wait, no. You said you hadn't been on any second dates."

"I haven't," I say a little glumly. "All of the men have been perfectly nice, all pleasant looking in their own way. But no chemistry. *None*."

Rachel tilts her head. "Then why the Cinderella mode? You only ever revert to that when you've got a crush."

I take a deep breath. "Okay. Here's the part where you're going to want to dust off your best lecturing voice."

Rachel taps her throat and hums like a singer warming up her voice. "Okay, ready. Hit me."

"There's this guy on the app I really like talking to. But . . . we haven't met."

"Hmm." She purses her lips. "No lecture *yet*. But why not just meet him and see if you have chemistry?"

I bite my lip. "He's not really available."

"Then what's he doing on a dating app?"

"He didn't actually sign up for the app. He was at a friend's bachelor party, and I guess one of them got drunk and thought it would be hilarious to steal his phone and set up a profile on his behalf."

"Okay, but if you guys hit it off—"

"He has a girlfriend," I interrupt.

"Ohhhhhhhh," Rachel says, eyes widening. "That's tricky. Wait. You're having a cyber affair! With a cheater!"

"I'm not. I'm really not!" I repeat at her look. "And he's not a cheater. After we matched, I messaged him, and he explained right away what had happened and that he wasn't looking for a relationship. If he were looking for some sort of weird Internet affair, would he have told me about his girlfriend right away?"

"No," she admits. "But then why are you two still talking?"

"We're just friends," I say, shrugging. "After he replied to my message, I replied saying no problem, and then *he* replied, and then *I* replied. Somewhere along the line we discovered both of our first crushes are from *Empire Records*—"

"I'd forgotten about that! You *loved* A.J."

"Still do," I say with a nod. "He had a thing for Corey. We both live in Manhattan, we're both highly suspicious of oatmeal, we both lost our dads to lung cancer four years ago, we both put mustard on our scrambled eggs—"

"So gross."

"We don't, however, like the same ice cream, apparently."

"You're smiling that smile again," Rachel says. "Sweetie. I'm not buying this *just friends* thing. You're in love with this guy."

"I've never met him!"

Rachel's lips purse as she shifts Matteo to her other shoulder. "Does Lily know about this?"

"That I sometimes message a male friend? Why would I bring it up?"

I don't add that I *might* have mentioned it, if the last time we had dinner Lily had not been going on and on about a documentary she'd just watched about online predators.

"Caleb?"

"Yes," I say sarcastically. "My younger brother loves to hear all about his sister's love life."

"Ah-ha! So it *is* a love life."

Whoops. I definitely walked right into that one.

"Did I tell you Caleb moved to New Hampshire?" I ask in an admittedly lame attempt to change the subject.

"Yes, and I *still* don't fully comprehend moving out of a rent-controlled loft in SoHo to a barn in New Hampshire, but quit trying to distract me. Does *anyone* know about this? I need backup that this is nuts."

"Keva knows," I say, referring to my friend and upstairs neighbor.

Rachel looks away with just the slightest flinch, and I feel instant regret. She and Keva have met a couple of times and get along, but I sense she's sometimes jealous of the friendship.

"Hey," I say gently, pushing my finger into her forearm. "You're still First Bestie."

"I know," Rachel says with a sigh. "It's just another reminder that living out in freaking Queens means I don't get to see you as often or get to know the daily details of your life anymore."

"But you have a *yard*," I point out.

"It's more like a patch of dirt, but . . ." Rachel grins. "Yeah, I have a yard. My mother is scandalized. I swear, half the reason she wanted me to bring the kids into Manhattan today was because she's worried they're not getting enough concrete."

Amy and Sammy, Rachel's other two kids, are spending the day with her mom in Morningside Heights, which is the *only* reason I'm not fussing more that I don't get to see my de facto niece and nephew. Grandma trumps best friend, and though I'm careful not to mention it, Rachel's fears about Astoria being too far away from her old life aren't totally unfounded. It's at least an hour by train, which means I don't get to see her or her family as much as I'd like.

Rachel gives me a sly look. "What do you think he looks like?"

Medium height. Wiry build. Longish brown hair, warm brown eyes. Big smile.

"I haven't thought about it," I say casually.

"Uh-huh. Liar. In these fantasies of yours, is he by any chance a musician and a Sagittarius?"

"Okay, that's impressive," I admit.

"I know," she says, looking mollified to have best-friend status restored. "But you forget that we spent all of middle school and most of high school discussing our future husbands in very specific detail." She pauses. "*Damn*, I was far off."

"You mean your hot Puerto Rican husband isn't a blond surfer named Dustin? Get out."

"Oh, Dusty. What might have been," she says dreamily before turning back to me. "Aren't you worried your mystery guy could be, like, a hundred? With gout and gingivitis? What if his *girlfriend* is a caretaker at his nursing home, and the most action he gets is a sponge bath?"

"That would be fine," I say primly. "I can be friends with someone of a different generation."

I send out a silent plea to SirNYC. *Please don't get sponge baths.*

Rachel takes a last bite of her sandwich, then scrunches the paper wrapping into a ball with a sigh. "I want to warn you about catfishing, but honestly this is too adorable, assuming you don't do anything dumb. Like agree to meet him in a back alley."

I let my eyes go wide. "Wait, so I shouldn't have wired my life's savings to his overseas account and then given him my home address when he asked to see my panty drawer?"

"Aren't you funny. Here, want to give my arms another break?"

"Absolutely," I say, taking the baby and kissing his head.

"How'd you manage to escape with this one? Grandma Becca would have snatched him right up."

"Oh, she tried. But though she'd die for her grandkids, she's not big on diapers, so all it took was a casual mention of eruptive poops to secure some Auntie Gracie time." She gives a slight sniff. "Joke's on me though. I think he's just backed up my lie with a very real diaper situation that needs to be addressed."

"You want to change him at the shop?" I ask, gathering up the remnants of our lunch as she straps Matteo to her chest in some fancy-looking sling thing.

One of the best things about the champagne shop I own and run is that it's just across the street from Central Park.

Rachel gives me an apologetic look, and I shake my head before she can speak. "You need to get back. Don't worry about it.

"I do. Ugh. I've become one of *those* moms, huh? Can't be apart from her Littles for more than two hours."

"Those are the *good* kind of moms," I reassure her as we begin making our way toward the west side of the park.

Rachel tosses our garbage into the green trash can and links her arm in mine, careful not to jostle Matteo. "You don't have to walk this way with me," she says, checking her watch. "Doesn't the shop open at noon?"

"Josh and May are there. Plus, I need to get flowers for the counter, and Carlos on Seventy-Fourth and Broadway always has the best ones."

"Damn, I miss those pop-up Manhattan flower carts. Almost as much as I miss May. Give her a squeeze for me, it's been way too long. And wait, who's Josh?"

"Newish hire. Mostly helps with inventory and stocking, but it's sweet to watch him overcome his shyness customer by customer."

"I'm surprised you even know what shyness looks like. Have you ever met a human being who didn't instantly adore you?"

"Blake Hansel, fifth grade."

"No, he just *really* adored you, in the pull-her-pigtail kind of way," Rachel says as we exit the park and step onto the bustling Central Park West sidewalk. We embrace, careful not to smoosh the baby between us.

I pull back and give Matteo a proper goodbye, unapologetically inhaling his sweet baby smell, mingled with—yep, there's the eruptive poop. "Goodbye, handsome. You sure you don't want to run away with me?"

"You, young lady, will text me more often," Rachel orders with a pointing finger as she begins walking backward uptown toward her parents' place in Morningside Heights.

I salute in acknowledgment and wave goodbye.

The second my best friend's back is turned, I pull out my phone to see if I have more messages from him.

Okay, fine. So maybe I'm a *tiny* bit in love with a man I haven't met.

My dear Lady,

Pistachio gelato, you say. That's my mother's favorite, on the very rare occasions she lets herself eat food with actual flavor or calories. Alas, I confess the often-added green food coloring creeps me out.

Yours in renewed devotion to sorbet,

Sir

_____

To Sir, with alarm,

Did you just compare me to your mother? Not sure how I feel about that . . .

Lady

_____

My dear Lady,

I hear it now. I take it back and reassure you that in no way do I think of you as my mother.

Yours in apology,

Sir

two

Okay, a little bit about me.

My name is Gracie Cooper and I'm thirty-three years old, middle child, New Yorker by birth and choice, proud owner of a champagne shop called Bubbles & More, and I love my life.

Now, let's be clear. I can't quite claim it's the life I'd envisioned as a kid, and let me tell you, my best subject in school was daydreaming, so I did *a lot* of envisioning my future life. And no. Thirty-three does not look like I thought it would.

I don't have the husband or the kids. I live in a cramped one-bedroom walkup, not the tastefully renovated brownstone. In my daydreams, my parents were happily running their champagne shop together, and I was a world-famous artist (hey, if you don't dream big, why bother!). My brother and sister lived close by, happily married with their own kids, and noisy family dinners would ensue every Sunday like clockwork. It's also worth mentioning that in my daydreams, adult Gracie's hair and boobs were a lot less flat.

Alas. Destiny served up something a little different.

My mom died young—a hit-and-run accident a few blocks from our home in Brooklyn when I was seven. Four years ago,

I was gearing up to tell my family I'd been accepted into art school in Italy, only to be blindsided by my dad's Stage IV cancer diagnosis and his bluntly stated dying wish that Bubbles stay in the Cooper family.

My sister and brother hadn't exactly leapt at the chance to take over, and I was already Dad's de facto protégée in the wine business, so no art school.

Instead, I'm a shop owner who paints only as a hobby. And considering my sister and I have drifted apart and my brother moved to New Hampshire on a whim . . . no weekly family dinners either.

Not the life I imagined, but it *is* a good life. And I'd be lying if I didn't take a lot of pride in what I think of as my personal superpower: the ability to accept and embrace things as they *are*, not as I wish they could be.

Which is why it's so darn frustrating that there's one dream I can't seem to let go of, one area in my life where my heart refuses to settle for anything less than the daydream:

The guy.

No matter how many times I put myself out there, no matter how many dates I go on—and believe me, there have been plenty—I can't let go of the sense that when I see him, I'll know.

Rachel calls it my Cinderella mode. I call it having high standards.

Okay fine, *really* high standards.

But why *should* I settle for less than a stomach-flipping meet-cute or the kind of romance you see in old movies and listen to in Frank Sinatra songs?

My Sagittarius musician with the floppy brown hair, crooked smile, and dad bod is out there. I'm positive.

Which brings us full circle back to SirNYC.

It's crazy, even in my own head, but messaging with him is the closest I've ever felt to *it*. Which is why I can't quite give up our unusual friendship, because until Prince Charming shows up? Sir is *really* good company.

Turning onto Amsterdam Avenue, I head toward Carlos's flower stand, taking my time and letting myself enjoy the energy of New York City coming out of summer hibernation. Two taxis narrowly avoid a fender bender, communicating their dislike with that classic blaring NYC horn. Two old ladies gripe about Zabar's raising the price of smoked fish. An ambulance siren wails in the distance. A lanky man in headphones sings a pitch-perfect rendition of "Wait for It" from Broadway's *Hamilton*.

I smile at the city's soundtrack. *Home.*

I was born in Brooklyn, but I've lived in Manhattan since I was eight. And I mean no disrespect to the fine residents of Prospect Heights, but this bustling rush of the city, with skyscrapers and people way too close together . . . *this* is my New York.

After my mom was killed, my dad moved us to Morningside Heights, a West Harlem neighborhood right on the Upper West Side border. Manhattan represented a fresh start for all of us. A chance to navigate life without my mom in an apartment that didn't have her stamp all over it. A new school district for me and my siblings, plus an easier commute for my dad to the Midtown shop.

None of it was easy. I still remember the horror of having to ask my dad to pick up pads on his run to the bodega while my older sister was at summer camp. And of course I missed my mom like crazy. I still do.

But something weird happened when my dad drove the U-Haul over the Brooklyn Bridge and we were instantly surrounded by skyscrapers. Something inside me seemed to click—a sense of rightness.

I once went on a date with a guy from Toledo (who by the way did *not* have that click of rightness) who said Manhattan either got into your blood or made your blood run cold. It's a little graphic and gross, but he's not wrong. I was in the first category.

On Amsterdam, the crosswalk signal is red, but like any true New Yorker, I pay attention to actual traffic, not signals, giving a friendly, semiapologetic wave to the NYPD officers who either missed, or more likely, turned a blind eye to my jaywalking.

The flower cart is right where it always is, and I smile at the short man currently rearranging bouquets in their little buckets of water.

"Good morning, Carlos!"

"You are late." He scowls at me.

"I know, I know. I had a hot date with a beautiful baby." My gaze is skimming over my options, and I'm disappointed, but not surprised, to see fewer choices than usual. Typically I get here as early as I can on Monday mornings to get first pick of the arrangements, but today it's well after lunch. I reach for a bouquet of cheerful yellow roses, but Carlos swats my hand

and bends to lift something out of what seems to be a secret stash tucked behind the cart.

I gasp at the lavish bouquet. "Oh, it's stunning."

"Pauline, she made this late last night, told me not to give it to nobody but Ms. Gracie."

"You saved it for me?" I inhale the fragrant blooms. I'd have never thought to combine freesia, sunflowers, and hot pink roses—which is exactly why I'm not a florist.

"Wasn't easy," he grumbles good-naturedly.

"I definitely don't deserve you," I say, shifting the bouquet to the crook of my left arm, and with my right, fish around in my back pocket for the cash I'd shoved in there specifically for this purpose.

I hand over the bills to Carlos, making him promise to keep the change and thank Pauline.

Just as I'm putting my remaining twenty back into my pocket, the wind picks up, and it escapes.

"Oh damn." I don't usually curse, but much as I love this city, its busy streets aren't exactly an ideal place to drop a twenty-dollar bill on a breezy day. I make an awkward lunge for it, but miss as the wind picks up again, taking it farther down the sidewalk, only to be stopped by the toe of an expensive-looking male dress shoe.

I reach for the fluttering bill, but the owner of the shoe beats me to it, bending and plucking up the twenty with long fingers.

I smile in relief, already reaching for the money as my gaze travels up the tall length of a navy suit, conservative maroon tie—

Our eyes lock, and I freeze. Aqua eyes—yes, that's a thing—stare back at me, his surprised expression matching my own shock.

All that noise I mentioned? The New York City soundtrack? It all fades away until it's just me, him, and Frank Sinatra singing "Summer Wind."

Well, whatever, it's almost October, but close enough.

"*You*," I say, my voice quiet.

I've never met the man. I've never even seen him before. And yet I *know* him. My heart knows him. *This* is my Prince Charming, my love at first sight.

Turns out, he's not an average-height, musically inclined Sagittarian, with long brown hair, brown eyes, and a dad bod after all. He's tall, lean, and serious, with black hair, sharp features, and Tiffany-blue eyes.

The man has his phone in his hand, but slowly he slips it into his suit pocket, all of his attention on me. He doesn't take his eyes away from my face, and when our fingers brush as he hands me the twenty, his eyes narrow ever so slightly, as though in puzzlement. "Who are—"

"Sorry, babe. Thanks for waiting." A tall woman with thick honey-colored hair appears by Prince Charming's side. She holds up a Stuart Weitzman bag. "They had over-the-knee boots in dove gray. I couldn't resist."

He blinks and looks her way, and the Frank Sinatra record playing in my head scratches and cuts off midtrack. *Moment over.*

The woman glances my way and gives a curious smile. She's pretty. A perfect blend of approachable, wholesome, and

Manhattan chic, all freckles and big white teeth, in a dress that looks like it was custom made for her statuesque, curvy frame.

Of course. Of course a man like that would be with a woman like this, pure sophistication and polish.

Not a five-two shop owner who names pigeons, who had eggs with mustard for breakfast, and who probably has . . . I glance down. *Yup.* Baby spit on my shirt.

I check their fourth fingers. No ring—yet—but I'm sure it's only a matter of time.

The woman's gaze drops to the flowers in my arm, and her smile grows even prettier. "Those are gorgeous. Where did you get them?"

I snap back to reality and go into autopilot, smiling back at her. "Carlos here has the *best* flowers," I say, turning and gesturing to the stand where he's helping an older man pick out what I like to imagine are flowers for his longtime lady love. Ooh, or maybe a *new* lady love—a second chance for both of them as they help each other heal after losing beloved spouses.

Frank Sinatra starts to sing in my head again, albeit faintly. *Whew.* Still got it.

"*Look* at those hydrangeas," the pretty woman is gushing. "I need those in my life."

She walks past me without a second glance, thick hair and Stuart Weitzman bag swaying as she begins perusing Carlos's wares.

I glance once more at The Guy and find he's studying me as though I'm a puzzle he can't quite figure out.

Look all you want, buddy. You're taken.

I smile. A bright, platonic smile that's the equivalent of a friendly punch on the shoulder. "Thanks for this." I lift the twenty-dollar bill, which, had things gone differently, I totally would have framed and hung above the mantel of our first home together.

Alas. He's Prince Charming, all right.

Just somebody else's.

Huh. I'd been so sure that had been The Moment.

Oh well. I begin humming "New York, New York" to myself and pull out my phone, smiling when I see I have a new message on MysteryMate.

At least I still have Sir.

To Sir, with curiosity,

Do you believe in love at first sight?

Lady

My dear Lady,

Of course.

Yours in dying of curiosity why you ask . . .

Sir

three

By the time I get back to Midtown, I've pushed the man in the fancy suit with teal eyes to the back of my mind and heart, where he will sit on the shelf alongside my other perfect, unattainable men, like Prince Eric from *The Little Mermaid*, Mark Ruffalo's character from *13 Going on 30*, and of course, A.J. from *Empire Records*.

The bell that's been on the front door of Bubbles & More for longer than I've been alive jingles as I let myself into the shop, and my mood boosts a little when I see we have three customers. It's not a lot. But it's better than the *zero* customers we had three years ago.

The shop's always been small, the revenue modest. But even though I worked at the shop throughout my twenties, I hadn't realized how much we'd been struggling—none of us kids had—until I took over after Dad died. Not that it was Dad's fault. The reality of modern life is simply that people want to be able to order their vodka, their cabernet, and their Prosecco all from one place. They want to be able to do it online. And they want it delivered to their doorman while they're at work.

For all Dad's adamancy that customer service, product expertise, and neighborhood loyalty would carry the day, the numbers had said otherwise.

And though I can't claim that champagne or being a shop owner has ever been my dream the way it was Dad's, the desire to protect a loved one's dream and legacy is a powerful motivator. In the months following Dad's passing, I swapped art school in Italy for business school here in the city, taking all morning classes so I could be here when the shop opened at noon. I changed the store's name from Bubbles to Bubbles *& More* and expanded our inventory. In addition to being a champagne store, it's now also an upscale gift shop—the type of place you pop into on your way to a dinner party, bridal shower, or birthday gathering to get a bottle of celebratory bubbly and a little something fun for the host or guest of honor.

Slowly but surely, the store began making money instead of losing money, but I'd be lying if I said I wouldn't sleep easier if we were just *a bit* more comfortably in the black. Or if I said I didn't have flickers of resentment that while my dad had left the shop to *all* of us—Lily, Caleb, and myself—my siblings have been off busily chasing their dreams, while only I fought to preserve Dad's.

It grates more than I want it to.

But I wasn't the only one who practically grew up here. I wasn't the only Cooper kid who did homework on the little table in the back corner, who spent early teenage mornings restocking before the store opened, who could recite the difference between dry and extra dry champagne long before I could legally drink it. And all of three of us had been in the hospital room during Dad's last days when he'd requested that we carry on his and Mom's legacy.

But those flickers of regret and resentment are just that—flickers. Like I said, making the best of what I'm handed is my superpower, and I'm proud of what I've achieved. Proud most of all that in addition to the pretty journals, rose-gold staplers, and cute cocktail napkins, the most popular items are the paintings we sell in the little "art corner" I set up.

My paintings.

In fact, while one of the customers is getting a rundown from my employee Robyn on the nuances of Franciacorta in our Italy section, the other two are in the art corner, gushing over one of my more recent works—a leopard-print martini glass with a sassy red lipstick mark on the rim. Originally, I stuck with mostly champagne-themed prints. But they sold so quickly I decided to try painting all types of wine, not just sparkling. Then cocktails. Then fancy coffee, with the foam shaped into little Empire State Buildings, as many of our customers are tourists looking for NYC souvenirs.

That each new idea for a painting seems to sell better than the last is a point of pride and frustration, mainly because the operation of the shop leaves me with little time for painting.

Carlos's flowers still cradled in my arm, I head toward the cash register, where a sixty-year-old woman is reading one of the historical romances she's never without.

"Thank God," she says, not looking up from her book as I reach for last week's bouquet, which has seen better days. "Those other ones were starting to smell like rot."

"Which, clearly, you fell all over yourself trying to remedy," I say good-naturedly.

She peers at me over the top of her purple-rimmed reading glasses, then slowly removes them, letting them rest against her impressive bosom, held in place by a hot pink chain.

I tilt my head and point to her right ear. "Is that a rabbit's foot?"

She flicks the fuzzy red thing with a coral nail. May Stuckley has always been a cacophony of color and unique fashion sense. She's also the closest thing I have to a mother, almost as much a part of this store's legacy as my *actual* mother, and one of the most important people in the world to me.

"Rabbit's feet are lucky," she informs me.

"Then why only one?" I ask, since her left earring is a glittery pineapple.

"The asymmetry suited my mood," she says, putting an ancient-looking bookmark with a little tassel into her book about an earl and his bride. "How was Rachel and her little one?"

"Good and adorable," I answer. "Everything okay here? Thanks again for opening."

May shrugs. "I didn't, really. *She* was already here," she says, "lowering" her voice to a whisper that's somehow louder than her usual voice. She tilts her head in the direction of Robyn, who's still going on about the pinot bianco grape.

"I hear that tone. I'm ignoring that tone," I say over my shoulder, heading toward the back to swap the wilting flowers for the new ones.

"You don't like her either," May mutters.

I swallow a sigh at the familiar refrain. I don't *dislike* Robyn, though I swear, the woman sometimes acts like it's her life's mission to ensure that I do. Robyn Frank was my dad's last hire before he got sick—a sommelier I expect he hoped would be the ticket to ending the store's struggles. I'll grant that the woman knows her stuff when it comes to sparkling wine. Not just your basics, that cava from Spain is the best bang for your buck and that only sparkling wine from the Champagne region of France should actually be called champagne. Robyn takes it to a whole other level. She knows the flavor differences between a chardonnay-forward sparkling and a pinot noir–forward sparkling. She knows the different types of soil, the flavor effect of a vine's location on a cliff, what happens to a grape in the sun, and a host of other things that I honestly do not give a fig about, but some of our customers seem appropriately impressed.

She's brilliant. She can also be difficult and condescending.

I enter the "cave" at the back of the store. My parents called it that for as long as I can remember because it's windowless and constantly cold for the sake of the wine inventory that's not fancy enough to warrant a spot in the refrigerated wine locker, but still needs to be kept at fifty-five degrees.

I'm still hot from my walk, so the blast of cold air is welcome. I drop the old flowers into the trash—May's right, they do stink—and rinse out the crystal vase. It's got a fairly decent sized chip from when eleven-year-old Caleb thought bouncing a golf ball off the counter in a wine shop was a good idea, but I'll never get rid of it.

I don't have many memories of my mom, and those I do

are a little foggy. But I do remember her painstakingly arranging yellow flowers—her favorite color—in this vase every week. Using the same vase makes me feel close to her, even if I like to change up the flower colors a bit more than she did.

The flowers don't need much arranging—Pauline is a genius like that, creating "plop and drop" bouquets that look good without any fussing. I admire the gorgeous flowers once more as I carry the vase back out into the shop. All three customers have left, and May's disappeared, so it's just Robyn, who makes a very big show of putting away the enormous wine tome she's reading before giving me her attention.

She's the type of woman who's in her late twenties but looks older—on purpose, I'm pretty sure. She always, and I do mean *always*, wears a black blazer over a white button-down, paired with black slacks. Even in the middle of summer. Her straight brown hair is cut to her chin, and she once informed me she has it trimmed every twelve days, *precisely*, to maintain "the line." Completing the look is her trademark brownish-red matte lipstick that somehow emphasizes the fact that she never smiles.

I sense that she's gearing up for a complaint and try to beat her to the punch. "Any takers on the Franciacorta?" I ask, knowing that spreading awareness about the excellent Italian sparkler is one of her pet projects of late.

Robyn shrugs. "He said he'd be back later to pick up a bottle."

I feel my heart sink a little bit. They *never* come back later to pick up the bottle. I wish I could say that losing one customer doesn't matter, but even though the store's better off than it was a year ago, we can't afford to let our few customers leave empty-handed.

"Some ladies bought your cocktail picture," she says. "*I* had to ring them up, because May decided to take an early lunch."

"Hey, that's great," I say, ignoring the swipe at May. "I'm glad that picture found a good home."

She shrugs. "How can you possibly know it was a good home? They could have been murderers."

"Yes, I'm sure that's the hallmark of murderers. Buying leopard-print-themed watercolors while out shopping with their friends."

"I didn't really get it," she says, missing or ignoring my sarcasm. "Drinking out of a patterned cocktail glass is almost as bad as drinking out of a patterned wineglass. You can't properly assess the color, and if you can't assess the color, your nose doesn't know what to expect."

I glance at my watch. "Isn't it your lunch break?"

"*Past*," she says, grabbing her purse. "May couldn't be bothered to check the schedule, so I had to cover."

"I've got this," I say, because really, it doesn't take much to run a shop with zero customers. "Take an extralong one and enjoy the sunshine. It's a lovely day."

"I'll be back in exactly one hour," Robyn says.

"Fantastic."

I pick up my phone, settling on the stool with the intent to write to Sir when the bell jingles.

Praying it's a customer and not Robyn back to inform me that it's *not* a lovely day and that she *doesn't* enjoy the sunshine, I stand, ready to offer assistance if needed.

The man stops to inspect the Bargain Bubbles bin at the front of the shop. Usually people rummage a bit to see the different labels and prices, but he studies them without moving.

Then he turns toward me, and my *welcome, customer!* smile freezes before it can start, because I find myself staring into a familiar pair of aqua eyes.

My dear Lady,

Where do you fall on serendipity? Fate? Destiny? Or is it all mere coincidence?

Yours in inquiry,

Sir

_____

To Sir, with careful consideration,

Hmm. I don't believe in coincidence . . .

But I'm learning the hard way that while serendipity may be real, it's not always pleasant . . .

Lady

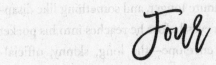
Four

You found me, is what I think.

"You," is what I say.

The surprise in his eyes tells me he's as shocked to see me as I am him. The slight line between his thick dark brows tells me he's not quite sure what to do about it. He looks around, as though wanting to verify he's where he's supposed to be. "Hello. I'm looking for the owner."

Ugh. You don't own a shop without quickly learning that "I'm looking for the owner" almost always means a complaint or a tacky sales pitch.

Still, I force a bright smile. "I'm the owner. How may I help you?"

The line between his eyebrows becomes a full scowl. "You're a member of the Cooper family?"

I try to hide my surprise. Some of our longtime regulars know we're a family-run shop, but it's not something we advertise. And this man is definitely not a longtime regular.

Maybe if we were, he'd be married to me instead of dating that other woman, and we'd have aqua-eyed babies . . .

Oh dear, Gracie. Pull it together.

I keep my smile in place and nod. "I'm Gracie Cooper."

He stares at me a minute longer, and something like disappointment flickers in his eyes before he reaches into his pocket and pulls out a white envelope—the long, skinny, official-looking kind, not the cute *just thinking of you!* greeting card variety that we sell in this very shop.

"I came to deliver this in person," he says. "It seems the ones we've sent by mail have gotten . . . lost."

The second I see the envelope, recognizing the discreet navy logo that's become the bane of my existence over the past couple of months, I roll my eyes. "You can take that right on back to your boss."

He lifts his eyebrows. "My boss?"

"I'm assuming you work for Sebastian Andrews?" I say, irritatingly familiar with the name that's been the signatory of every letter.

The man stares at me coolly before replying. "I *am* Sebastian Andrews."

No doubt the man delighted in surprising me with his name as much as I enjoyed surprising him, but make no mistake: it is a surprise.

In fact, for a moment my entire world seems to tilt sideways in denial. How can it be possible that in the span of an hour I went from thinking this man was the love of my life to learning that he represents everything I hate about business?

Sebastian Andrews works for the V. Andrews Corporation, the company we lease the Bubbles space from. For the past three months, they've been making repeated, unwelcome offers to buy out the five years remaining on our ten-year lease, each version of the letter colder and more stern than the last.

"Of all the men," I mutter. "It had to be you."

Mr. Andrews blinks his remarkable eyes. "Pardon?"

Oops. "I said that out loud?"

"You did. You weren't aware?"

I wave a hand. "I thought I'd outgrown my tendency to blurt out everything I'm thinking, though thoughts are really a bit of a revolving door, don't you think?"

"Hardly."

"Shouldn't they be though?" I persist.

"Shouldn't what be?" he asks warily.

"Wouldn't life be more interesting if everyone was a bit more open?" My question's rhetorical, but this stiff man in his formal suit seems to consider it seriously.

"Actually, I disagree entirely. If everyone spouted their every thought to every person, you'd remove the unique joy of getting to know one person in particular."

It's a wonderfully valid argument, and my opinion of him goes up fractionally, even as my annoyance with him increases tenfold.

"Is there something I can help you with? A nice bottle of Tattinger to celebrate your girlfriend's new dove-gray boots?" I say with my best customer service voice.

His eyes narrow in warning. "I'm not here to purchase anything."

"Just what all shop owners love to hear."

"You received my company's letters," he says. It's not a question.

"I did, yes. Very high-quality stationery."

"Did you open them?"

"Some of them."

His jaw tenses. "And the rest?"

"Went to a *very* special in-box."

Mr. Andrews looks weary. "Let me guess. The trash bin?"

"No!" How very insulting. I gesture him around the counter, and with a sigh, he complies.

I regret my decision immediately, because it's a small space, and it brings him near enough for me to smell his cologne, something smoky and masculine.

I point down to the paper shredder we keep beneath the counter, indicating the pile of crimped white scraps. "We only use this for the most *special* of papers."

Unamused, he turns his head toward me and our eyes lock. Again, I feel that strange pull I felt on the sidewalk, that whisper of white doves and happily-ever-after. Only now that pull is also laced with frustration, both that he has a girlfriend and that he's a corporate robot who seems to think nothing of trying to bully a beloved forty-year-old family shop out of business.

Mr. Andrews steps back around to the other side of the counter. I stay where I am, and when he puts the latest letter he's brought with him on the counter between us, it feels like a line in the sand.

He and I engage in a silent battle of wills for what feels like minutes, though I'm sure it's only seconds.

"Open it," he commands.

"No, thank you. Not interested."

His palm resting on the counter twitches, his fingers thrumming one at a time in plain irritation. "You don't even know what it says."

"It says that you want to put us out of business."

He has the nerve to roll his eyes. "Don't romanticize it."

"Don't *romanticize* it?" I repeat, outraged. "I assure you, my concern for my employees' livelihood, my own livelihood, is extremely grounded in facts and logic."

"If that's the case, you owe it to your employees and yourself to seek the best option for them."

"Oh, and closing my business will somehow achieve that?"

"We've put together a very compelling offer. Something you'd know, had you found a less *special* place for my letters."

"Oh, I can think of a less special place," I say sweetly.

His fingers drum once more, faster this time, more irritated, and it fills me with . . . something.

I'm a middle child through and through, accustomed to being the peacemaker, to making everyone comfortable, to charming the conflict out of tense situations, but for the first time in my life, I have no desire to remove the tension in this moment. Mr. Andrews can go ahead and *choke* on it for all I care.

Unfortunately, I'll be deprived of the pleasure of watching that, because the jingle of the bell indicates a new arrival. I glance at the front door, recognizing one of our regulars, and lift my hand in greeting.

"If you'll excuse me," I say. "Paying customers require my attention."

"Ms. Cooper, all I want is five minutes to discuss a business offer that would be beneficial to both of—"

"Understood," I pick up the letter. "I'll be sure to set this aside for review later."

Holding his gaze, I lean down and feed the letter into the shredder. If our previous standoff had been a silent cold war, the shrill clatter of his offer being diced into a million pieces is a warrior's cry.

He shakes his head, having the nerve to look disappointed in me.

"If you ever need some help fulfilling your sparkling wine needs," I say under my breath, "I'd be delighted to point you to one of our competitors on Sixty-Fourth and Columbus."

As far as parting remarks go, it's not exactly gold, but I'm fairly pleased to at least have gotten the last word as I round the corner and head toward my customer without so much as a glance his way.

"Nicola, how are you?" I ask.

Nicola Cirillo is a publicist who lives in one of the fancy high-rises nearby and who's in the shop at least once a week or so. She's in her midforties, maybe even a very well-maintained fifty, and lives to entertain, frequently buying cases at a time for brunches, trivia nights, watching the Oscars, Super Bowl parties, etc.

Most of our regulars know what they like and buy the same label over and over, much to the chagrin of Robyn. Nicola, on the other hand, is always on the lookout for something new. Robyn's going to be ticked she missed a chance to sell her Franciacorta.

"How'd your vintage game night go?" I ask, recalling the reason for her last visit.

"It was a huge hit, thanks. Fun fact, tipsy Candy Land is more fun than you'd think. And you were so right on the New Mexico bubbles, by the way. Who knew the Southwest could produce that sort of quality?"

"We just got some more cases. Can I grab you a couple bottles?" I'm increasingly aware that Mr. Andrews missed my hint to leave and is now roaming the shop, pretending to browse.

"No," Nicola says, running a well-manicured hand through her long blond hair as she surveys the front display of sparkling rosé. "I've got sort of a last-day-of-summer itch. I want a fun, pink Monday wine. Just for me." She says it with a grin.

A lot of customers have the last-day-of-summer itch, which is exactly why I'd set up the summery display Nicola's currently perusing at the front of the shop. In addition to the pink wines that scream *sip me in the sunshine*, I've also pulled together some summery hosting goodies: pool blue cocktail napkins, glittery fruit wineglass charms, and champagne bottle stops in bright pops of color.

I'm secretly itching to replace the whole thing with my fall display, but when Nicola makes a delighted sound at a corkscrew shaped like big Audrey Hepburn sunglasses, I know I've got at least another week to try to move the summer inventory.

"You have this one cold?" she asks, putting a finger to the foil of a Rotari Rosé.

"Pretty sure I do," I say. "Let me double-check."

A quick trip to the refrigerated section affirms that I have the bottle cold, and that Sebastian Andrews is still lurking. I glare at his profile, but he's too busy pretending to study a bottle of Dom to notice.

I return to Nicola, still holding the sunglasses corkscrew as she surreptitiously steals glances at Mr. Andrews.

"Wow," she mouths silently to me. She fans herself.

I know. But just wait till he opens his mouth and ruins it.

Guess I can have inside thoughts after all.

"Anything else?" I ask, lifting the bottle in question.

"Just that. Oh, and this," she says, handing me the corkscrew. "I don't need it, but it's too cute to pass up."

I feel a swell of professional pride at her words because the "don't need it, but too cute to pass up" crowd was exactly the clientele I was banking on when I'd decided to add the *& More*.

See that, Mr. Andrews? We're doing just fine.

Sort of.

Nicola absently picks up a little tin of outrageously priced mints and slides them toward me as I ring her up. The mints, wrapped in black and hot pink packaging, are shaped like champagne flutes and taste vaguely like vanilla. I carefully hide another victory smile. Displayed in a crystal bowl at checkout, they're one of our most popular impulse buys.

I place her bottle of champagne in a sturdy, skinny white paper bag and slip the corkscrew and mints into the sides. That is another of my improvements. We used to use the industry standard brown paper bag slipped into an equally ugly plastic bag. After taking a class on branding at business school, I decided that one way Bubbles & More could differentiate itself was to create an experience of luxury, even after you walked out the door, carrying a sleek, attractive bag that you could carry to happy hour with friends without ruining your outfit.

"Thanks so much," Nicola says, blowing me a kiss. "You know I'll be back. I always am."

She glances in Mr. Andrews's direction one last time, then I hear the tinkle of the bell, and I'm alone again. With him.

Sebastian takes his time coming around to the counter, and I'm unsurprised to see he has no wine bottle in hand. And it goes without saying he's not the type to pick up cocktail napkins while he's here. I lift my eyebrows. "You did see the no loitering sign on the door, yes?"

There isn't one, but it doesn't matter, because he ignores the question and thoughtfully picks up one of the mint tins from the bowl. "Eight dollars for a tiny thing of mints."

The mildness of his tone is more insulting than a snide intonation would have been. "They're one of our best sellers."

"I'm sure." He sets the tin back in the bowl carefully. "Does the profit margin cover the cost of the fancy bag?"

He can't know it, but his question hits me right in the deep, dark, endless hole of worry that I reserve for those 3 a.m. anxiety attacks.

Or maybe he *does* know it, because his gaze is level and steady. He sees too much. Almost as though he knows the margin on the mints is next to nothing, and the cost of pretty white bags that are sturdy and well made enough to entrust a hundred-dollar bottle of champagne is astronomical. And no, not covered by the mints.

I channel my older sister's snootiness and look down my nose at him, which I secretly think is rather impressive because I'm five two and he's at least six feet. "Little luxuries are a crucial hallmark of the Bubbles brand."

"I'm sure. And profit? Long-term viability? Your own financial security? Are those hallmarks of the Bubble brand as well?"

I'm not particularly prone to anger, but I feel an unmistakable bite of indignation at his condescension. "You overstep, Mr. Andrews."

He concedes the point with a nod. "I do. I apologize. But brick-and-mortar stores are rapidly becoming a thing of the past in *all* industries, Ms. Cooper. There's no shame in admitting that this shop will never make you rich."

"I would never be ashamed to admit that," I say quietly. "In fact, I say quite proudly that there are more important things in life than being rich."

He doesn't ask *what things?* but his expression tells me he's thinking it.

Those unfairly beautiful eyes cut to the fresh bouquet I was holding when we first met, before I realized he was a shark in a really smart suit.

"Enjoy your flowers," he says, somehow managing to make it sound like a parting shot as he turns and strides toward the door.

The bell tinkles with his departure, and I stare blindly at the beautiful blooms, hearing everything he didn't say.

Enjoy your flowers. But they won't save your shop.

To Sir, with plausible deniability,

Do you think a good maiming is ever justified? Kidding, mostly.

Lady

My dear Lady,

She has a dark side! Consider me intrigued. Noisy neighbor? Cheating boyfriend? Toxic relative?

Yours in the cone of silence,

Sir

Workplace frustration. Some people are so . . . so . . . there are no words.

Lady

Ah yes, something I understand all too well myself. The word you're looking for is actually two: *utterly provoking.* Some people are utterly provoking.

Yes! That is it exactly. This individual has me utterly provoked.

Same. Same.

Five

My sister, Lily, is one of those beautiful people. As a kid, I'd been unaware of it. As a teen, I'd been a little jealous. As an adult, I've learned there are more important things than outer beauty.

Just kidding! Rarely do I look at her without thinking *damn you, gene pool, you didn't play fair!*

Don't get me wrong, I'm just fine with what I see in the mirror. My hair's a little on the thin side, but I've learned that if I don't let it grow beyond my collarbone, I can keep it from looking scraggly. Naturally it's somewhere between light brown and blond, though I lean into the blond with a little help from CVS hair dye. I got my dad's strong chin and my mom's blue eyes and petite stature.

But then there's Lily. She also got Mom's blue eyes, but with Dad's dark brown hair and insanely thick lashes. Hers are the sort of eyes described as "startling," whereas my high school boyfriend once described my eyes as "bluish?" I think the question mark at the end had been the most insulting part.

Lily's also tall, curvy, and has that sort of commanding

presence where she owns a room just by stepping into it. The current room being Bubbles & More.

"Hey!" I say in surprise, looking up from my laptop where I'm reviewing our numbers for the week. They're not good.

I shut the laptop and go to hug my sister. "I didn't know you were stopping by."

"I had to pop into Bergdorf's," she said, inspecting my summer display. Her nose wrinkles just for the tiniest moment, and she straightens the cocktail napkins into a tidy stack, unaware of the fact that I'd fanned them out just so for a reason.

I feel a flicker of irritation, but I let it go. It's much harder to push aside the flicker of hurt that the only reason she'd stopped by was because she was already in the area.

What happened to us?

Lily and I have always been different, but we were also close. She's seven years older, fourteen when my mom died, and in a lot of ways, she fulfilled the mom role in those early years. It was Lily who put mac and cheese on the table when my dad worked late, helped me muddle through long division, and stroked my hair after a nightmare.

Even after she married her high school sweetheart and moved out of the apartment, we talked daily, and she still helped out at Bubbles on weekends. But by the time I was well into my twenties, both Lily and Caleb had moved on with their own lives. I'd been the lone Cooper kid helping Dad with Bubbles, and neither sibling had questioned whether or not I wanted to be there.

"How are things going?" she asks.

"Great!"

Lily studies me closely, the same way she used to when she'd ask how my social studies tests had gone.

I'd lied back then too, and she'd always known it.

She scans the shelves of sparkling wine. "You switched Italy and Spain."

"Cava's been having a moment," I say with a shrug. "Though if it were up to Robyn, anything that isn't real champagne would be in the back of the store, behind a black curtain."

She sets her chic black bag on the counter and heads into the back corner to look at the art. "You've expanded the art selection."

I shrug, feeling a little self-conscious. "Lots of tourists popping in on weekends looking for souvenirs to take home. It was getting a little crowded."

"That's so great!" she says enthusiastically, picking up one of my more recent pieces—a tiny pink fairy using a ladle with a bow on it to sip champagne from a coupe.

"I always forget how talented you are," she muses. "You could always draw, but these are . . . remarkable." She scans the handful of works. "They're all yours?"

"Yeah. I tried bringing in other artists' work, but . . ."

Lily's smile is smug and proud. "They didn't sell as well as yours?"

I spread my hands and grin. "What can I say? I'm a marvel."

"You are," she says, carefully setting the fairy piece back down. "I've always been jealous that you have a hobby you're actually good at."

A hobby. Some of the joy I feel at her praise fades. It's never occurred to my family that my art could be more than a hobby, and it chafes more than I should let it, considering I've never told them I once wished it could be more.

When she turns back toward me, she's still smiling, but there's something else there—concern mingled with hesitation.

"Just say it," I say with a sigh.

"I don't want to overstep."

That's a first.

"Lily."

My sister takes a deep breath. "Alec went to this fundraiser at the Guggenheim on Saturday."

First I note the choice of words with interest. *Alec* went, not *we* went. Fundraisers at museums have always been Lily's bread and butter. My brother-in-law, not so much. He's a bigwig about town, but also an introvert. He'd take a bourbon and a book over a social outing any day, so the fact that he went without being dragged by Lily is . . . unusual.

"Apparently he ran into the son of one of New York's most famous families . . ."

I close my eyes and pretend to snore, waiting for her to get to the point.

"The Andrewses."

My eyes snap open. *No.* Not those Andrewses. It's a common last name, one of the most common last names, surely . . .

"Gracie." Lily's voice is soft, chiding. "How could you not tell me and Caleb that there'd been an offer to buy out Bubbles? It's our company too."

And yet, this is the first time you've stepped foot in here in months. Caleb hasn't been here in years.

But my frustration at my siblings pales in comparison to my anger at Sebastian Andrews. The insufferable man didn't get what he wanted from me, so he went to my brother-in-law?

Of all the chauvinistic, *snakelike* moves . . .

"I'll kill him," I mutter.

Lily's eyes widen slightly. "Whoa. What am I missing?"

I lean heavily against the counter. "It's a really long story."

"I've got time," Lily says, lifting a finger. "Hold."

She goes to the refrigerated section, sliding open the glass door, and comes back with a bottle of Pol Roger. She digs into her purse, comes out with a sleek black envelope, and pulls out a fifty-dollar bill. She starts to go around to the cash register, opening the laptop. I know she means to record the transaction, but I place my palm on the laptop. The store's numbers are still up, and they're ugly.

"I'll take care of it later."

She blinks in surprise at the sharpness of my tone, but she shrugs, then picks up the champagne and begins twisting the wire cage with expertise. Dad always used to joke that his kids knew how to open champagne bottles before they were off their milk bottles, though he was old-fashioned in that he didn't let us drink the stuff until we were eighteen, and then only little sips of whatever he was tasting.

The real lesson came on our twenty-first birthdays, when he'd open a bottle of Dom Perignon. Our lifestyle was modest. We were not Dom Perignon people. But on twenty-first birthdays, we pretended we were, and it was magical. Though in hindsight, it was rather unfair of him. Having something as decadent and fabulous as Dom as your first proper glass of champagne is rather ruinous. The sparkling wine that is in my budget can't hold a candle to it.

I pull out two of the glasses we keep in the tall, old-fashioned curio behind the checkout stand. My dad had taught us sparkling wine should be drunk out of proper stemware, or not at all. Robyn supports this philosophy wholeheartedly, which I suspect is half the reason she got the job. She'd wooed Dad with talk of nose and bouquet and aroma and *damaging the bubbles*.

Personally? I think it's rubbish. Sure, the science probably stands up, but as far as I'm concerned, wine isn't about science. Wine—especially the sparkling kind—is about the *moment*. A ten-dollar sparkler sipped out of plastic cups to celebrate an engagement beats the pants off a three-hundred-dollar bottle of Cristal sipped from a crystal glass by someone bored by life.

"These are new," Lily says admiringly, picking up one of the tulip glasses I've pulled from the cupboard. She expertly fills one glass, letting the bubbles get to the very top, but not overflow, before moving to the second. She repeats the process until the bubbles settle to drinkable level.

I've had this particular champagne—a reliably good one for the price—dozens of times, but I lift it to my nose anyway out of habit. Lily does the same, but neither of us swirl the way we might with a robust cab. It's *sacrilege* to swirl bubbles.

"So," she says, taking a tiny sip of the champagne and fixing me with her big-sister stare. "Sebastian Andrews."

"Ugh. The worst. A troll in a suit."

Her dark eyebrows lift. "I've met him. Just briefly, a mutual acquaintance's wedding last year. But he seemed perfectly polite. And even as an old married lady, I can see he's ridiculously handsome."

"He's ridiculous all right. Ridiculously *smug*, thinking the world should bow to his every whim."

"His current whim being buying out the lease here?"

I nod.

Lily sips her champagne. "I hope you told him to suck it."

"Lily!"

"What? It's our family legacy. It pisses me off that some corporate drone, even a handsome one, just waves a big check and doesn't think twice about trying to snuff out a locally owned business."

I sip my wine to carefully hide my resentment. It's one thing to defend a family legacy with words. It's another to have to be the one putting in the work.

Oblivious to my frustration, Lily picks up one of the fancy mint tins and smiles. "You ever wonder what Dad would think about all the stuff you added?"

"All that *stuff* is the only thing saving the business."

She looks up in surprise, though I'm not sure if it's at my words themselves or my tone. I've always been the one who had smoothed out the sharp edges of my stubborn father, bossy sister, and impulsive brother. I used to take pride in being the good-natured, easygoing one in the family, but lately I wonder if I haven't also been a bit of a doormat.

"Is the store doing okay?" she asks.

"It's doing okay," I say, purposefully repeating her word. "But it's not doing great. It's not even doing *good*. For all Dad's insistence that a personal touch and exceptional customer service will save the day, it's hard to fight the power of the Internet and free delivery."

She taps her nails. "We could lean into the e-commerce space. Have Caleb redo the website, let people buy online."

"I've asked Caleb about five times to redo the website," I say, sipping the champagne. "He always says he'll get to it, but in between his paid projects and playing lumberjack . . ."

"But—"

"I know you want to help," I cut in gently. "But respectfully, I'm the one who's been managing the day-to-day. I'm the one who'll figure out how to handle Sebastian Andrews."

I don't tell her that a body bag is involved in my fantasies.

"You're right." She holds up both hands. "You're absolutely right. Let's change the subject."

"Thank you," I say, reaching out to squeeze her hand. "How's the renovation coming along?"

Two years ago, Alec and Lily vacated the little one-bedroom they'd rented for more than a decade and bought a three-bedroom apartment in Tribeca. Despite the new place's fancy address and upscale building, the former owners had questionable design tastes: lots of black in the kitchen and a powder room I can only describe as construction-cone orange. The sink had been shaped like a butterfly.

To say that the renovation was an ambitious project is an understatement, but Lily, being Lily, had attacked it with a vengeance. The neon-orange powder room would be painted over with soft grays and mauve accents, the black lacquer cabinets in the kitchen replaced with white wood and glass, the stainless-steel kitchen island redone with black marble. The second bedroom would be turned into a guest room, the third into an office or a nursery.

The part of me that can't wait to be an aunt is *really* curious about the destiny of that third bedroom, but I'm not entirely sure how to ask. I know they've always wanted kids—they've been trying to conceive the natural way, but they've also tried a variety of fertility treatments. But I also know that biology is a real bitch and that while forty-year-old women *do* have babies, it's often not an easy road.

"The renovation's great," she says, though the smile doesn't come anywhere close to reaching her eyes. "But I don't want to talk about my boring married life. Tell me about your single life. Seeing anyone?"

"Trying to," I mutter.

She smiles. "Still chasing the fairy tale?"

I lift my glass. "Still chasing."

"Maybe Sebastian Andrews is on the market," she says teasingly.

"Nope." I take a generous swallow of wine. "He's got a gorgeous girlfriend with the best hair and freckles you've ever seen."

"I bet not as gorgeous as you."

I snort. "On a good day, I'm cute, but hardly Sebastian's type, nor he mine."

She purses her lips. "Don't get mad at me for going all Big Sister on you, but . . . do you ever think maybe it's time to let go of your type? I'm all for knowing what you want, but if your Mr. Perfect hasn't shown up by now . . ."

"He's out there," I say lightly, trying not to think of the very unavailable Sir.

She looks like she wants to argue, but instead studies her champagne, twisting the glass this way and that, the tennis bracelet Alec bought her for their twentieth anniversary last year sending a little kaleidoscope of light over the counter. "Have you talked to Caleb lately?"

"A few texts," I say casually, knowing it's always bothered Lily that she and Caleb aren't as close as he and I. "Hey, let's set up a video chat with the three of us. I miss his stupid face."

She smiles. "Me too."

I pull out my phone to text him, and a half hour later, I hug Lily goodbye, a sibling chat on the calendar for the following week.

Checking my watch, I see it's a little past closing time and flip the Open sign, trying not to feel despondent that in the entire time Lily was here, not a single customer came in.

I turn back to the shop, and for a moment I take it in as a stranger might—as Sebastian Andrews might. I look around at the well-stocked shelves, lined with bottles that are carefully dusted every other day to disguise the fact that we don't move all that many. The dark hardwood floors are clean, but scuffed, in a way I hope looks timeless, when in reality, there's no room in the budget to have the wood refinished.

I head back to my laptop, intending to dig back into the dismal books with the vain hope that I've miscalculated something—double counted an expense or miskeyed a sale.

Instead of opening my computer, I pick up the framed photo that sits on the shelf behind the register. It was taken on my dad's birthday, just a couple of weeks before my mom was killed. We'd gone to the Jersey Shore for a beach trip. My dad had splurged on a new camera, and for this tiny moment, he had managed to get the four of us—three kids and Mom—to pause our sandcastle building, Popsicle eating, and beach reading to pose for the photo.

My mom's blond hair is windswept, and her sunglasses as big as her smile, as she crouches on the sand, gathering the three of us close to her. Lily and I are in matching purple swimsuits and smile obediently at my Dad's *say cheese* command. Six-year-old Caleb, armed with a plastic bucket and shovel, is scowling at having his work on the sandcastle moat halted for the ten seconds required for him to stay still.

It's not a perfect photo, but it *is* a perfect moment.

I use it as fuel to remember why I'm doing this, why I'm keeping the shop alive, when sometimes it feels blisteringly hard. The photo is a reminder that this space, this store, is not about the numbers on my laptop that are lower than any of us want them to be. It's about family. The Cooper family.

If Sebastian Andrews has a problem with it, he can bring it to *me*, not my brother-in-law.

I'm not tipsy—not quite, but I've had just enough wine to feel all fired up and ready for war. I reach for one of the letters from Sebastian Andrews—the first one, and the only one I didn't shred. I reread it, even though I know what it says. They want to buy out our lease and would be interested in a conversation if we could contact them at the below number to set up a time and place that's convenient for us.

Convenient my ass.

There's nothing even remotely convenient about someone trying to swipe your job out from under you.

I'll be contacting them all right, but not for the reason Sebastian Andrews thinks.

I reach for my cell phone and dial the number, but before hitting the call button, I set my phone aside and pull out a ballpoint pen and a yellow legal pad. It's 9:45 on a Thursday, which means I'll get voice mail. Best get my talking points ready.

    ✦ *Bubbles is not for sale.*
    ✦ *If you have a problem with that, you can bring it up with me, not my brother-in-law.*
    ✦ *How can someone with such beautiful eyes have such an ugly soul?*

I scratch that one out.

    ✦ *Go to hell.*

I circle that one. It's my thesis.

Maybe I'm a little tipsy after all, but it gives me the courage I need to hit dial, clear my throat, and stand up straight as I prepare to give my little speech.

I'm listening for a generic recording and the beep, so the rough "Sebastian Andrews" catches me off guard.

"Hello?" The gruff male voice says after a moment of silence, clearly impatient.

"Oh crap, is this your cell number?" I blurt out. Okay. Maybe a little tipsy after all.

Now it's him who's silent. "Who is this?"

"Gracie Cooper. I'm so sorry to call so late. I thought this was your office number—"

"It is."

I frown and look at the clock on the wall, where the hour and minute hands are both—you guessed it—champagne bottles.

"It's nearly ten o'clock."

"Well, thank God you called to let me know, Ms. Cooper. I'd never have known the time without this call."

I ignore his sarcasm and sit on the stool, pulling my heels up to rest on the wooden slat and resting my elbows on my knees. "Do you always work this late?"

Another moment of silence, as though he's trying to decide whether responding to me is worth his time.

"No," he answers finally. Then, "Sometimes."

"You answer your own phone? I'd have thought you'd have a fleet of beautiful assistants in high heels to handle such menial tasks."

"My assistant's name is Noel, and he leaves the office at six. Is there something I can help you with?"

"Oh, right." I pick up my notepad and clear my throat dramatically.

"Here we go," I hear him mutter.

"Bubbles is not for sale." I say it clearly, enunciating each word.

"Nobody's asking you to sell the company, just give up the

space. You can always relocate, perhaps to a neighborhood with cheaper rent. Did you read *any* of the letters before destroying them?"

I ignore the question and look down at my notepad, my irritation bubbling fresh all over again.

"Oh yeah," I say, tossing the legal pad onto the counter and warming to my topic. "How dare you go around me to my brother-in-law!"

"How dare I?" He has the nerve to sound bemused.

"I run this shop. Not Alec. Ergo, I make the decisions."

"Ergo."

I frown. "You keep repeating me. Am I being unclear?"

"No, no. Just enjoying your word choice."

"Well, see if you can focus on the context," I snap. "How would *you* feel if I went around you to go to your sister-in-law to discuss business."

"I don't have any siblings, and I'm not married. *Ergo*, no sister-in-law."

"Why not?"

"Why don't I have any siblings? You'd have to ask my parents."

"No, why aren't you married?" I clarify. "Your girlfriend is super pretty," I add when he doesn't respond.

Yep. Definitely a little drunk. I pull out the snack basket and grab a peanut butter protein bar.

"Believe it or not, my qualifications for proposing marriage go beyond *pretty*."

I tuck my phone under my ear and open the cellophane, taking a bite as I consider this. "What are your qualifications?"

"Is this why you called, Ms. Cooper? To discuss my personal life?"

"No, that wasn't on my list."

"You have a list?"

"Yup." I pick up the pad once more. "Number one, not selling. Number two, you had no business going around me to my brother-in-law. Number three . . ."

"Number three?" he prods when I don't continue.

I read the third item on my list about his beautiful eyes that I'd crossed out.

I skip that one. I'm not *that* drunk.

"Number three," I say, smiling. "Go to hell."

Sebastian—when did I start thinking of him as just *Sebastian?*—heaves out a sigh.

"Look, to clarify, I didn't *go around* you to your brother-in-law. I'm not the villain in a mediocre legal drama. We happened to be at the same event, in the same general vicinity. A mutual acquaintance made introductions, asked if we knew each other. In an effort to make conversation and find common ground, I mentioned that I'd recently met you. He asked for context, and I said I had a business proposal for you. I assure you, had I known I'd be harassed with a late-night phone call over it, I'd have never mentioned your name."

I finish the rest of my protein bar as I listen to his explanation. It checks out. I still hate him.

"This isn't harassment," I say, crumpling up my wrapper and tossing it in the trash.

"No?"

"Nope. Harassment would be sending repeated letters to a

local business that clearly wants nothing to do with you and then stalking them at their place of business when you don't get the response you want. *That's* harassment."

"No," he says with measured patience. "That's business."

"Not the way *I* do business."

"No, I've seen the way you do business," he snaps. "Instead of acknowledging that your business model is passé and your customer base shrinking, you delay the inevitable by selling ten-dollar trinkets and cutesy Tinker Bell paintings, and then slapping a generic modifier onto your business name."

Cutesy Tinker Bell paintings.

It stings *way* worse than Lily dismissing my art as a hobby. I'm not sure if it's the champagne, the protein bar, or the combination, but suddenly I feel slightly queasy.

"I apologize, Mr. Andrews. I should not have called so late," I say quietly, my righteous fury all burned out, replaced by heartbroken weariness. "Have a nice evening."

"Ms. Cooper—"

If I hear a tinge of remorse in his voice, I ignore it and hang up.

To Sir, with bruised feelings,

Do you ever let a comment slip under your skin that
shouldn't? The sort of jab from someone you don't even
like that you should really brush off, but instead it keeps
you up at night because it . . . hurts?

Lady

———————

My dear lady,

Given the hard-to-define nature of our correspondence,
this is perhaps overstepping, but I confess my knee-jerk
reaction to your note was to ask for a name and address
of the offender. Duels are still a thing, right?

But alas, that would be a bit hypocritical of me. I too have
been up at night, though not for something I heard but
for something I said. A rash, spontaneous comment I wish
I could take back.

Perhaps whomever hurt you feels the same regret? And if
not, let me know about that duel . . .

Yours at dawn,

Sir

Six

I've moved apartments a few times in the past eleven years, but I've never switched neighborhoods. The city sometimes likes to pitch this neighborhood as Midtown West or Clinton, but make no mistake: we locals call it by its proper name, Hell's Kitchen.

It sounds gritty as hell (pun intended), and while it has its moments, for sure, the neighborhood's not nearly as rough as it used to be. Not to say it's glamorous—I can't afford glamorous, but neither do I particularly *want* it.

I currently live in a walk-up on Fifty-Fourth Street between Ninth and Tenth Avenues, in a cute little one-bedroom apartment. Does it have sleek granite countertops, central air, and a glass shower? Certainly not. Does it have brick walls, a window AC unit that does the trick, and a whole lot of character? Yes. Yes, it does.

If I could change one thing, I, like most New Yorkers, wouldn't say no to more space. My living room doubles as my art studio, which means I can't watch TV without first moving my easel, nor can I sit on the couch without first removing the plastic sheeting that protects the faux leather from flecks of paint.

It's become my normal though, so I don't really notice so much anymore. Whenever I start to feel a little crammed, I remind myself that I'm an artist in the city, and then I feel pretty darn lucky. Well, not a *working* artist—that generally implies I'd be able to live off my art, which I can't.

But knowing people buy things I create? There's really no high like it, and it makes up for the inconvenience of having to turn sideways and slink against the wall to scoot around the easel to open the window—something I do the second I get home on a sunny afternoon, because the apartment has the distinct whiff of *cat*.

"Cannoli, darling, what in the world did you do to your litter box?"

The black-and-white cat jumps onto the back of the sofa and stares me down. *I did a thing. Clean it.*

"For being the runt of the litter, you produce a lot of output," I mutter, scratching him behind the ears as I scoot around my work in progress to deal with the joys of being the owner of an indoor cat.

I pause and study the watercolor on my easel. It's girly to the extreme. A pink cocktail in a traditional martini glass, with a whimsical New York City skyline in the background. It's got distinct *Sex and the City* vibes, but the watercolor and not-quite-to-scale skyline make it feel softer, the type of scene where you wouldn't be all that surprised to see a fairy with turquoise wings sitting atop the Empire State Building. Actually—I like that idea. I might add exactly that.

Cutesy Tinker Bell paintings.

"Little does Sebastian Andrews know I take that as a compliment," I say, glancing at Cannoli.

The cat pauses in cleaning his paw. *He didn't mean it as one.*

"I know, I know," I grumble.

I take care of my litter box duties and change out of my work clothes—a sunny yellow dress and clunky-heeled sandals—into gray joggers and a plain white T-shirt. I dated a sweet coder in college for about a year, and by far the best thing to come out of that relationship was discovering the joys of men's undershirts. Since I no longer have a guy in my life to swipe them from, I buy the soft and surprisingly affordable tees for myself.

It's too early for dinner, but I skipped lunch, so I pull out a loaf of bread. Since I'm out of turkey, and Cannoli calls dibs on the tuna, I make myself a budget-friendly peanut butter and jelly sandwich. Leaning against my counter, I take methodical bites and wonder what to do with the rest of my day.

I rarely take Saturdays off—they're one of Bubbles's busiest days. But Josh, my newest hire, has been asking for more shifts—and more responsibility—lately, so I'd begged off at three to let him handle the afternoon and evening crowds under May's watchful supervision.

Robyn's working too, which is an annoyance for everyone else, but for once, I'm grateful for her infuriatingly extensive champagne knowledge. Josh is a hard worker and great with the customers, in his shy, sweet way, but he doesn't know much about sparkling wine and is perhaps the only person in existence who actually seeks out Robyn's lectures. He even carries around a little leather journal and takes notes. It's very cute.

Three rhythmic knocks, inspired by Sheldon from *The Big Bang Theory*, tap on my door, and I grin, because there's only one person who knocks on my door that way.

Keva Page is my upstairs neighbor, fellow *Big Bang Theory* fanatic, and exactly the sort of girlfriend every adult woman needs. Not that I love Rachel any less, but there's something nice about having someone close enough to pop over whenever she feels like it. Keva filled the gap in my social life when Rachel moved to Queens. Keva is the brash, bold Miranda to my romantic Charlotte with less good hair.

I open the door, and she jumps back from where she'd been about to insert my spare key in the lock. She checks on Cannoli for me when I have to work late at the store. "Hey! You're home. I was just going to leave this on your counter." She waggles an open bottle of merlot in her hand. "I'm headed out to Cape May for a job and didn't want this bad boy to turn to vinegar while I'm gone."

"Ooh, beach trip! Jealous! You in a rush, or you want to come in for a glass?" I ask.

"Mmm, both," she says, rolling her red suitcase into my apartment. She hands me the bottle, then walks without hesitation to the cupboard where I keep my wineglasses and pulls down two. "Let's make it fast, but don't be chintzy with the pour."

"Wedding?" I ask as I pour the wine. Keva is the assistant chef for a catering company. Not the kind that brings in big bowls of potato salad and pigs in a blanket, but the *fancy* kind.

Saffron arancini, truffle crab dumplings, and homemade ricotta ravioli with arugula pistachio pesto are some of her latest masterpieces that I was all too happy to taste-test.

In addition to being crazy talented, Keva's the type of woman who crackles with energy, who declares red her favorite color and *owns* it. Her lips are always a bright cherry red, and on days when she doesn't have to work, her nails match. In silent protest to her boring white chef uniform, she's informed me that she only ever wears red underwear, which probably explains at least in part why her love life is so much better than mine.

"Fancy engagement party," she answers, sipping the wine and pushing her trademark silk headband—also red—a little farther back into her dark hair. It's tucked into a tidy bun now, the way she wears it for work, but I know the second the job's over, she'll pull out the elastic and let her amazing black curls do their thing.

She moved into the building about a year after I did, and we met when her pasta was delivered to 4C (my unit) instead of 5C (hers). Thinking it was my own Chinese delivery, I accepted it before realizing it was the wrong one. I'd taken the bag upstairs to deliver it to her myself, and hearing *The Big Bang Theory* theme song through the door, decided to make whoever was on the other side my new best friend.

She picks up my sad-looking peanut butter sandwich, and shaking her head, scolds me. "It's not even *homemade* peanut butter."

"I don't know how to get this through your gorgeous head, but not everyone makes their own nut butters."

"They should." She helps herself to a bite and licks jelly off her thumb. "Okay, I've got a boring train ride with my irritable boss ahead of me. To get me through, tell me the latest on your sexy pen pal, and if it hasn't evolved to the point of cybersex yet, lie to me and pretend it has."

"God, I hope I'm not that hard up," I mutter. "Am I?"

She finishes my sandwich. "Well, let's see, your last date was . . . ?"

"A respectable two weeks ago."

"Uh-huh. And last kiss . . . ?"

I don't reply—I'm too busy trying to remember—and she shakes her head. "I repeat. Cybersex."

"For, oh, I don't know, the *thousandth* time, Sir and I are just friends. Also, quit saying the word *cybersex*. I don't think that's a thing anymore."

"Oh, it's a thing," she says with a little smirk as she finishes her wine. She glances at her phone. "Damn. I've gotta run, or Grady's going to start with the lectures."

"Speaking of kissing and sexy times . . ." I waggle my eyebrows. Keva and her boss, Grady, have an intense I-hate-you-so-much-but-I-secretly-want-you vibe going on, and the rom-com lover in me is not-so-patiently waiting for them to get to the good stuff already.

"I'd rather eat imitation crab than hook up with Grady," she says with enough disgust to let me know that imitation crab is as low as it gets in Keva Page's book.

I sigh. "So, neither of us is getting any."

"I didn't say that." She winks.

Maybe I should invest in some red underwear . . .

Keva grabs the handle of her suitcase and swats my ass before heading to the door. "Put on *Big Bang*, finish your masterpiece, and then *do* the big bang, even if it's virtually. That's an order."

She blows me a kiss and closes the door. Shaking my head, I sip my wine and decide to do two out of the three.

To Sir, with frustration,

Do you ever feel like the people closest to you are the ones who get you the least?

Lady

_____

My dear Lady,

Quite often.

Yours in mutual frustration,

Sir

_____

To Sir, in follow-up,

Do you ever find that the person who gets you the *most* is a person you've never met?

_____

My dear Lady,

Yes.

Seven

"Oh my God." I lean closer and peer at my laptop screen. "Is that a goatee?"

My brother laughs and rubs a palm over the scruffy hair on his chin. "Yeah. What do you think?"

"I love it," I say at the exact same time Lily announces from the left side of my screen that she hates it.

It's a little after eight on Sunday, and we Coopers plus May are finally getting around to our family video chat. Lily from her apartment, Caleb from his house in New Hampshire, and May and me from the shop.

"It's really good to see your face," I interject quickly before Caleb and Lily can start squabbling. "Facial hair and all. Though I'm shocked. They have Internet where you are?"

My brother grins, taking a quick sip of his beer. "I rigged something together with two sticks and some fishing wire." His eyes flick away from me, presumably looking at Lily's head on his screen. "Where's Alec?"

My sister shrugs. "Work thing."

On a Sunday night?

Having poured us each a glass of sparkling brut from

Sonoma, May nudges me aside and takes her place in front of the laptop's camera, scowling at Lily. "You know, I can't think of the last time I saw that boy."

I smile a little at überserious forty-one-year-old Alec being described as a boy.

Another shrug from Lily. "You know how busy his job keeps him."

May has never tried to insert herself into our lives as a maternal figure, even after she and my dad started seeing each other. She let us come to her, and we all eventually had. Even Alec. And as far as May was concerned, once you wandered into her nest, you were hers for life, to peck at and to protect.

"Wednesday night," she announces. "You and Alec will come to my place for vegetarian lasagna. You too, Gracie. Caleb's off the hook, not because he's in a different state, but because I won't be able to enjoy my eggplant lasagna while looking at that thing growing on his chin."

"*Nooooooo*," Caleb says in faux despair. "Don't make eggplant without me!"

Lily hesitates. "May, I appreciate the offer, but I really don't know if—"

"Wednesday night," May repeats with finality.

My sister sighs a little, then nods before changing the subject. "Baby brother, did Gracie tell *you* that some big corporation is trying to buy the store. She certainly didn't tell me."

"Seriously?" he asks, looking stunned.

"It's not a big deal," I say, nibbling a piece of cheese. "Think of it more as a newly discovered virus that goes by the name of Sebastian Andrews. Symptoms include nausea, extreme annoyance, and random surges of anger."

"Sis!" Caleb sounds delighted. "Is this *ire* I'm hearing from Snow White? Did you finally encounter someone who doesn't fit into the fairy tale?"

Yeah. I haven't exactly hidden my fairy tale–junkie status from . . . anyone.

"No, no," I say, popping the rest of the cheese into my mouth. "He actually has a starring role. As the villain."

"A villain with a great butt," May adds.

I pivot to look at her. "You've never even met him."

"I googled him," May says pragmatically. She tips her head back to take a sip from her flute, her neon-blue guitar earrings swaying.

"And you searched for 'Sebastian Andrews's butt'?" I ask.

What results came up? I don't ask. But I want to.

"I don't care if his ass rivals J.Lo's," my brother interjects. "I hope you told him to go to hell, Gracie."

"I actually did tell him exactly that!" I say, feeling rather proud.

"Good," Lily says firmly. "I'm glad we're all on the same page about keeping Bubbles in the family."

My brother nods, but I feel May's gaze on me. "Gracie?"

"What?" I pick up another cheese, mostly to avoid meeting anyone's eyes, even via a screen.

"Are you all on the same page?" May persists.

"Of course we are," Lily says indignantly. "The store's more important to Gracie than any of us. She's the one there all the time."

"What choice did I have?" The words pop out before I can stop them, and both my siblings look bewildered.

I take a deep breath. "I didn't mean it like that," I say. "Bubbles is important to me, of course. It's just sometimes I feel like I'm doing all of the hard stuff, all alone."

May squeezes my hand. *Go on.* I squeeze back and smile, grateful to have an ally. I take a deep breath. "I'm not saying we should sell. I'm just saying I could use some help."

"Crap." Caleb drags a hand over his face. "I feel like a jerk."

"Well, yeah," Lily says. "How many times has she asked you to fix the website?"

"Oh, and I'm sure you've been falling all over yourself to stop by and help her restock inventory in between your weekly manicures," he shoots back.

"Guys," I say in my gentle but stern middle-child voice.

"Okay," Lily exhales. "Okay. What do you need, Gracie?"

I need to double the numbers.

I decide to start with something less intimidating. "Well, I know neither of you were thrilled when I changed things up. You hated the new bags, protested the addition of *& More*."

"Only because Dad wouldn't have wanted it," Lily says, and Caleb nods in agreement.

Oh sure. On *that* they see eye to eye.

"I get that," I say softly. "But as the one who does the books, I can tell you that that's when things started to turn around. And we need to turn them around even further. The mom-and-pop model our mom and pop subscribed to just doesn't cut it anymore. I'm open to ideas—"

"A new logo," Caleb cuts in, ever the graphic designer. "I know I protested that last time you suggested it, but you're right. The one we have now looks tired, and you can never underestimate the power of a good rebrand. I'll get to work on some mockups for that and the new website."

"You know," Lily says, "the other day I went to a cooking class with a couple of girlfriends, and they had wine pairings with it. I wonder if we could do something like that with champagne . . . ?"

"Yes!" I say excitedly, pulling out a notepad to write it down. "My friend Keva actually teaches cooking classes. I bet she'd help. These are good. What else . . ."

Thirty minutes later, I have a sizable list of ideas to save Bubbles and feel the lightest I have in months.

Watch out, Sebastian Andrews. I'm coming for you.

My dear Lady,

Do you ever sense a storm is coming but can't quite figure out the direction or the source?

Yours in severe weather predictions,

Sir

_____

To Sir, with umbrellas,

Absolutely, though I confess I'm having one of those glorious days where I *am* the storm.

Lady

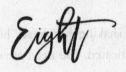

Eight

"Open." I open my eyes and stare into Keva's dark brown gaze as she gives my face a critical study. She waves her makeup brush in command. "Close."

I close my eyes as she resumes blending the eyeshadow on my right eyelid.

"Are you sure I shouldn't borrow one of your red dresses?" I ask.

"Not unless you can make these quadruple in size in the next hour." She unceremoniously thumps the top of my boob with a flick.

"Ow." I rub my breast as she whips away the towel that's been draped over my chest.

"Open," Keva commands.

I open my eyes once more, and this time after studying me, she nods in approval. "You're ready."

"And you're *positive* on the dress?" I ask, unfolding my legs from their cross-legged position on my bed. "It's not too . . . princessy?"

"Look, it's your favorite dress, right?" she asks, putting a fist on her generous hip.

"Yes. But it's not particularly sophisticated. I was picturing—"

She's already shaking her head, her bun wagging. "You don't need sophisticated. You need *power*. And there's nothing more powerful than a woman wearing her favorite dress because she knows she looks *good*."

I open my mouth to argue, but she points at me. "Stand."

I do and let her guide me to the full-length mirror I've leaned in the hallway outside the bathroom because my bedroom barely fits my bed and dresser.

"Oh wow," I say when I see myself. She's right, the dress is one of my favorites. It's a sort of pool-water blue, with an off-the-shoulder neckline, fitted bodice, and short full skirt.

My face, however, is . . . a masterpiece. I look like *me*, but more badass. She's done something to make my eyes seem bluer, more direct, yet you can't tell I'm wearing makeup.

"I know, right?" Keva says smugly. "You look like Veronica Mars meets alternate-universe Cinderella."

"I was going for Olivia Pope," I admit.

Keva shakes her head. "All wrong. He'll be *expecting* an Olivia Pope move. He won't see this coming, and it'll knock him on his ass."

"Well, I do like the sound of that," I say, heading back into the bedroom and pulling a pair of beige ballet flats from the shoe rack hanging over the closet door.

Keva bats them out of my hand and they drop to the floor. "Nope, those." She points at a pair of hot pink high heels. I bought them to match a bridesmaid dress for a college friend's wedding and haven't worn them since.

"You want a *little* Olivia Pope," she explains.

"There's zero chance I'll make it the two avenue blocks wearing those. I wouldn't even make it two regular blocks."

"Which is why you're taking a taxi."

I snort. "Just to get to Columbus Circle? I'll have to hand in my New Yorker card."

"You'll have to hand in your *scrappy* New Yorker card," she corrects. "Today you get to be the other kind of New Yorker. The kind who takes taxis without blinking an eye."

She pulls a twenty out of her bra and hands it over.

I shake my head. "I'm not taking that."

"Because it's been nestled against my boob?"

"Gross. *Nestled?* And no, I don't want it because I won't take your money, especially not to take a cab a few blocks."

Keva rolls her eyes and unabashedly tucks the money into *my* bra.

Giving up, I sigh and pull out the pink stilettos. "Fine. Only because it's fitting that a twenty-dollar bill plays a role in this meeting."

Keva stares at me. "Huh?"

"Never mind," I say, remembering I never got around to telling her about the sidewalk meet-cute between Sebastian and myself when I'd accidentally miscast him as the hero of my story for a hot minute.

Now that I know he's the villain, and that I'm about to enter his turf, a secret twenty-dollar bill somehow feels like an appropriate power play.

I put on the shoes and then wince as they immediately pinch my feet. I'm going to need that cab after all.

Last night, instead of sleeping, I was envisioning how this day would go. I pictured *everything* in my mind, right down to what the Andrews Corporation headquarters looked like: my imagination decided a lot of glass and stainless steel.

Turns out, I was 100 percent right. The elevator alone looks like a spaceship, except instead of astronauts, I'm joined by men in gray and navy suits and women in smart dresses and tailored slacks.

The cliché about New Yorkers wearing only black isn't entirely untrue, and I'm feeling a little out of place in my bright blue dress and pink shoes until a middle-aged woman behind me in the elevator taps me on the shoulder.

"Excuse me," she says with a smile. "I'm dying to know—where'd you get your shoes?"

"Oh!" I turn and smile back as I name the brand. "I do feel I should warn you, they're not terribly comfortable."

She sighs as the elevator doors open and she moves around me to exit. "They never are. Worth it though. Those are fabulous."

The compliment is a much-needed ego boost, and I feel increasingly confident about my impending meeting.

Sebastian Andrews, as one of *the* Andrewses, is on the second highest floor of the fifty-story building, so the rest of my elevator comrades are long gone by the time I step out onto the forty-ninth floor.

As with the lobby downstairs, the office space is very cool and modern—lots of white marble, white leather, and stainless steel—but it's all softened, rather surprisingly, by two stunning flower bouquets set up on either side of the large reception desk.

"Oh!" I say, forgetting to play it cool as I walk right up to the flowers and touch a hydrangea, which contrasts perfectly with pink snapdragons and yellow roses. "These are so pretty."

The black-haired man in tortoiseshell glasses behind the desk grins. "Aren't they? We used to order our arrangements from one of the generic corporate florists. Lots of white roses and lilies." He lets out a dramatic yawn. "Just a couple of weeks ago, Mr. Andrews found this local guy up on Amsterdam. He doesn't deliver, but I actually like to get out of the office to peruse the weekly selection."

I stare at him. Surely, he's not talking about *Carlos*.

If he is, I'm thrilled for Carlos and Pauline. These arrangements must have been wildly expensive.

But I'm irritated for me.

The thought of Sebastian Andrews and me getting our office flowers from the same place feels . . . irksome.

"You must be Noel," I say, extending my hand. "I'm Gracie Cooper. We spoke on the phone a couple days ago? I really appreciate you finding time on Mr. Andrews's calendar."

He looks surprised, as though nobody ever acknowledges his presence, much less his name.

"Yes, sure," he says, pushing his glasses up his nose and looking down at his computer screen. "I'm sorry I could only find a half hour, though honestly it's rare he has any time available this last minute."

"A half hour is all I need," I say.

"You're just a bit early, and he's on another call," Noel says. "Can I get you anything to drink while you wait? Water? Coffee? Tea? We've got a fancy espresso machine."

"I'm fine, thanks," I say, moving to the elegant but comfortable seating area. I've just settled in with an old *Citizen* magazine Man of the Year issue featuring Carter Ramsey, because who doesn't like to fantasize about a hot baseball player, when Noel says my name.

I glance up, and he nods toward the door. "Mr. Andrews is available."

I stand and pick up my purse, smoothing a hand over the back of my skirt to make sure I'm not living my *actual* nightmare of having it tucked into my underwear. Begging my already pinched feet to hang in there for another half hour or so, I enter Sebastian's office.

I was sort of hoping for something to pick on—a ghastly hunting trophy or a torture chamber of some kind, but the worst I can say is that it's generic. The desk big, the chairs black, the view . . . well, there's nothing generic about that.

"*Wow*," I breathe, my eyes scanning the view of Central Park and all of the Upper East Side behind him. I start to walk forward to the window, then pause. "May I?"

He gestures with an open hand toward the floor-to-ceiling windows in a way that makes me think I'm not the first to gawk. "Looking is free, photos are ten bucks."

"Oh, so the Tin Man makes jokes now," I say, stepping around his desk and walking to the window. Out of the corner of my eye, I think I see him check out my legs, my shoes. I carefully try to hide a smirk. And the butterflies.

"Tin Man," he repeats quietly, standing, though not coming any closer to me as I survey the stunning view of New York City in front of me.

I wave a hand in his general direction without looking his way. "You know. Tall. Thin. Controlled."

He says nothing for a long minute, though I feel him studying me, and the room suddenly becomes . . . charged?

No. He has a girlfriend. I have a . . . pen pal.

We hate each other.

Still, Sebastian surprises me by coming closer, stopping a respectable distance away, but close enough for me to smell his cologne, close enough to feel small next to him.

His left hand slides into his pocket as his right points ahead. "You can't quite see the sign through the construction scaffolding in front of it, but that's Bubbles."

I slowly turn my head to look at him. He hadn't even hesitated before pointing, as though he's already scoped it out.

"You were spying on me?"

"Yes," he says sarcastically. "I hurriedly stashed my telescope in the closet just before you got here."

His mention of Bubbles & More reminds me why I'm here, and shifting into business mode, I pivot and walk back around his desk.

"No pictures?" he asks with what might be a tiny fraction of a smile, but it's hard to know. I've never seen him smile.

"Can't afford it," I say sweetly. "Not with my outdated business model and 'cutesy Tinker Bell paintings.'"

If it was a smile I saw on his face, it's gone now.

"Ms. Cooper—"

I gesture for him to sit, even though it's his office. "May I speak?"

"Of course," he says, his tone as stiff as his posture as he resumes his place behind his desk, less man, more . . . suit.

I take a deep breath. "I was wrong to put your letters in the shredder without response. You were at least due a reply, a confirmation of receipt. I'd like to apologize for my lack of professionalism and respect for your time."

He's silent for a moment. "I appreciate that."

"You strike me as the type of man who doesn't act without first doing his research, so I expect you know that Bubbles is a family business."

"I do. I know your parents opened the store before you were even born."

I nod. "And both my parents are gone now. Bubbles isn't just a business for me, it's part of a legacy. *My* legacy. And it's one I plan to protect."

"Protect against big bad businessmen like myself," he says, leaning back in his chair as one palm rests on the desk, those long fingers ready to drum in irritation. The other rests on the arm of his chair, casual, but in a practiced way, as though he's studied how to look relaxed.

"I understand legacy, Ms. Cooper," he continues. "I understand family business. And because you strike me as the type of woman who's done *your* research, I'm sure you know that *this* is a family business as well. Do you have any idea what your stubbornness is standing in the way of? The magnitude of it, the number of people it would serve?"

"I too did my homework, and I know this company builds

high-rises. I also know that the last thing this city needs is another soulless skyscraper."

His jaw tenses in frustration. "And you're in the position to speak for the city?"

"Are you?" I shoot back.

"I've done my market research."

"I'm sure you've got a PowerPoint presentation bursting with graphs, but have you actually talked to people? Did you ever ask the people walking along Central Park South—right outside your window there, admiring the horses and carriages, delighted in their hot dogs—what they wanted from the New York City experience? Did you ever sit down with Jesse Larson or Avis Napier? Do you even know who they are?"

His aqua eyes flash with anger as he replies, his voice clipped. "This project won't have any ill effect on the horses, or the hot dogs. And yes, Ms. Cooper, I know Jesse Larson, former owner of Little Rose Diner on Central Park South, now owner of Little Rose Café in the East Village, recently written up with praise in the *New Yorker*. Avis Napier, former owner of The Central Park Spa, is now happily living in a brand-new beachfront condo in Florida, just a five-minute drive from her daughter's family."

A knot of unease has formed in my stomach, but I stand my ground. "Who are *you* to say Avis is happy? You bought her out and now you're just telling yourself whatever it takes to help you sleep at—"

He leans forward suddenly, all pretense of chill gone. He's all heat and anger. "Avis's daughter's name is Kathleen. She's married to Barry. Their son, Jon, just turned four, and their daughter, Monica, was born on the Fourth of July. When I spoke to her last Friday, she was out shopping for a birthday present for her grandson and leaning toward a talking microscope. As for Jesse, I highly recommend the mushroom and thyme scramble, though he's also recommended the ricotta French toast. And I intend to try that next time I go there for brunch, which will likely be this weekend."

He leans back in his chair, his posture relaxing slightly, but his intensity still crackling. "Yes, I talk to people, Ms. Cooper."

I keep my hands pressed to my lap, afraid that if I move them, they'll start shaking, because *I* feel shaken. Nothing about this meeting matched my daydreams. He's supposed to be a cold robot in a suit. I'm supposed to be the humane one who cares about people and my city.

Instead, I feel small. Selfish.

He checks his watch, his impatience plain. "What exactly is it that you came to tell me, Ms. Cooper? Or did you make the appointment merely to disparage my character?"

I try to gather my righteous anger, and while my voice isn't as strident as it was when I first sat down, at least it doesn't wobble or crack as I lift my chin.

"I know your business owns the building we rent from, which makes you, essentially, my landlord. But I also know that as long as we continue to pay the rent, you can't kick us out until the lease is up, which isn't for another five years."

Now it's me who leans forward. "I may have disparaged your character, but you belittled mine when you insulted my shop and *me*. You want to know why I made this appointment today? It was to *thank* you. Because you were right. I wasn't thinking big enough, and I intend to remedy that immediately."

His aqua eyes narrow. "Is that so?"

"It is," I say confidently as I stand. This time I know it's definitely not my imagination that his eyes track the hem of my dress where it falls just a *smidge* short of business appropriate, but when his gaze snaps up to mine, it's more irritated than ever.

"I do hope you'll consider *Bubbles & More* for all of your champagne needs," I say calmly as I pick up my purse and turn toward the door. "Though, if I might be so bold as to recommend you skip the art section—I don't believe you'd appreciate it."

My feet are screaming in the uncomfortable shoes, but I try harder than ever to hide it as I saunter toward the door.

"Ms. Cooper." His voice is right behind me. "Wait."

I don't slow my step.

"*Please.*"

Swallowing, I pause and force myself to turn back toward him. I regret it immediately, because he's followed me, and he's close. Close enough for me to smell that expensive cologne, close enough to see the precision of his tie knot, to feel the heat of his body . . .

That last one might be wishful thinking.

"What?" I demand, forcing myself to meet those remarkable aqua eyes.

He's staring down at me, looking frustrated, then squeezes his eyes shut and gives a quick shake of his head. "Nothing. Never mind."

I swallow again. "Okay then."

"Wait," he says again, touching my arm when I reach for the door handle.

This time when I turn back, he looks faintly embarrassed and lifts a fist to his mouth, clearing his throat slightly. "You have. Um . . ."

"What?" I say, more impatient this time.

His eyes drop to the vicinity of my chest, and before I can register what is happening, he's reaching out, the backs of his fingers brushing against my collarbone, and his touch seems to sear my skin with the desire for more.

Slowly his hand pulls away, and the sharp longing in my belly is replaced by a knot of humiliation when I see the twenty Keva had stuffed into my bra earlier that must have wiggled its way into visibility.

His lips twitch with the hint of a reluctant smile. "What is it with you and twenty-dollar bills?"

"Give me that," I snap, reaching out and grabbing the bill, much as I had the day of our first meeting.

I yank open the door, ignoring his soft chuckle as I storm out of his office.

There's an older couple chatting with Noel in the reception area, and the woman breaks off midgripe about her hot yoga class when she sees my shoes. "Oh my goodness. To be young again and be able to pull those off."

I'm beginning to *hate* these shoes. In addition to hurting like hell, they're preventing what could be a very sassy Walk Away.

Still, the woman looks kind and genuinely admiring, so I give her a sunny smile. "Thank you! Though I'll be honest, young or not, I'm about to go buy myself a pair of flip-flops because my feet are not enjoying their pointy-toed prison."

The woman laughs and points to her own feet, which are adorned with stylish white loafers. "I used to pride myself on wearing four-inch heels all day, then *boom*. I rounded the corner on fifty-five, and suddenly flats and wedges became my best friend."

Daaaang. If this woman is over fifty-five, I need to start investing in some serious eye cream, because I wouldn't have pegged her for a day over fifty. Her dark shoulder-length hair is thick and shiny without a hint of gray, her figure trim, and her skin has the healthy look of someone who's decided to embrace the natural aging process *and* sunscreen.

"I thought I was your best friend," the equally attractive man beside her says, glancing up from his phone with a wounded expression. Dressed in a light gray suit sans the tie, with a tanned complexion and deep smile lines, he's her perfect match, and I feel that usual tinge of delight and jealousy at seeing two people who clearly belong together. *I want that.*

She gives his arm a fond pat. "You're in the top five for certain, dear. Right in between my navy Tory Burch flats and Fendi sandals. It's a good place to be." Her pretty blue eyes move beyond me, her smile widening. "Sebastian, there you are."

"Mom. Dad." The gravelly voice from behind me sparks

an annoying tingle of awareness down my spine. Then his actual words register. These are his *parents*?

No. No way can two people so charming and pleasant produce *him*. They're all wide smiles and geniality. I don't think I've ever even seen his teeth.

But on closer inspection, I realize the woman's eyes aren't just blue. They're aqua blue, albeit a good deal more friendly than her son's. And while Sebastian doesn't particularly resemble his father, the elder Mr. Cooper has the same Ivy League airs and command of the room.

Belatedly, I realize that if these are Sebastian Andrews's parents, that makes them Vanessa and Gary Andrews, CEO and CFO of the company, respectively. I am annoyed to have to admit I'd stereotyped them by imagining them to be cool and aloof, instead of the type to cheerfully discuss shoes with a stranger.

"Thanks for pushing the schedule back for a late lunch," he says, and I glance at Noel, realizing that when he'd said Mr. Andrews had been able to move some things around, he'd pushed back lunch with his parents. To meet with . . . me?

It's nearly as puzzling as Carlos's flowers on his reception desk.

"Not a problem!" his mom says. "Will Genevieve be joining us?" I'm starting to ease around her to make my exit, but she looks my way once again. "Sebastian's girlfriend would go absolutely bonkers for your shoes."

Genevieve. The name fits her.

I smile politely. "I believe it. I don't think I've ever spoken about anything with as much affection as she had when she found a pair of over-the-knee dove-gray boots."

"Oh, you've met her!" Vanessa seems delighted. "Did Sebastian ever tell you how he and Genevieve met?"

I really don't want to know, but the way Sebastian shoves his hands into his pockets and scowls means he doesn't want me to hear it either.

I glance his way and grin innocently. "He's never said! But I love a good story."

"Well," his mother continues. "Gen's mom and I were sorority sisters back in the day, and we became the best of friends. Roommates, maids of honor, the whole deal. We even got pregnant at the same time. Genevieve was born just six days before Sebastian, and in the same hospital. We burped them together, changed them together. They were basically betrothed from birth. We never would have pushed them together if they weren't interested, of course, but you can imagine our delight when they hit puberty . . ."

"I got most of my gray hairs during that decade," Mr. Cooper says, running a hand through his thick head of salt-and-pepper hair that's a much lighter shade of brown than his son's.

"That's *adorable*," I gush with a wide grin at Sebastian. "My sister and brother-in-law are high school sweethearts. They've been married twenty-one years."

"You hear that?" Vanessa says playfully, raising her voice and glancing at her son. "*Married*."

She drags out the word for emphasis in a way that makes

me think it's not the first time they've had that conversation, and while I can't say I'm not a little curious about the situation, my exit is well overdue.

"Well, I'll let you get to your lunch," I say, lifting my hand for a little farewell wave. "It was nice to meet you!"

"Oh, I didn't get your name, you of the fabulous shoes."

"This is Gracie Cooper," Sebastian cuts in.

Vanessa Andrews's eyes flicker with something that looks like regret, telling me she knows exactly who I am and why I'm here, but I can't seem to hate her for it.

Maybe because all my hatred has been used up on her son.

"Well, it was lovely to meet you, Gracie."

"Same." I smile at her and her husband and wave at Noel.

I ignore Sebastian completely.

To Sir, with polite curiosity,

Do you have any pets? On paper, I'm a dog person. I love all that open affection and loyalty, the excitement they show when you walk in the door. And yet I have a cat. His name is Cannoli, he's completely indifferent to me, and I love him so. What do you think that's about?

Lady

_____

My dear Lady,
Perhaps it's *because* the cat is so indifferent that you love him so. There's something irritatingly irresistible about someone who won't give you the time of day . . .
Yours with armchair psychology,
Sir

Nine

As it turns out, Lily hadn't been exaggerating about Alec's busy schedule, because Wednesday dinner at May's got pushed out to Sunday.

"I thought you were going vegetarian," I say to May, picking up a little wheel of bacon-wrapped ricotta topped with chives and nibbling the salty deliciousness.

She pauses in stirring a pitcher of her legendary martinis. "Why would you think that?"

"Why else would you use eggplant in lasagna instead of beef?"

Her cocktail spoon resumes its stirring. "Because it's damned delicious."

May is wearing a printed wrap dress with bright red poppies and enormous grapefruit-slice earrings that somehow manage to look exactly right in her lime-green kitchen. She lives on Eighty-First and Madison in the stately, if dated, prewar apartment she bought with her second husband, and fourth Great Love, who'd died of a heart attack at age forty-seven.

May has had a lot of Great Loves, and while I still firmly

adhere to my belief in One True Love, I can't deny that I'm grateful my dad was her seventh Great Love, because it brought her into my life.

May never really talks about her financial situation, but considering I very rarely see her wear the same clothes—or earrings—twice, and the fact that she lives just off Madison, makes me think one of her Great Loves left her very well off.

Knowing that she doesn't have to work at Bubbles but continues to anyway makes me love her all the more, as does her taking a paycheck just like everyone else so I never feel like a charity case.

"So, what's going on with your sister and that boy of hers?" May asks.

I sigh as I chew the bacon and cheese. "You've noticed too, huh?"

"That our Lily's eyes never light up when she talks about Alec anymore?"

"Maybe they're just fighting."

May looks down at her cocktail pitcher, and the spoon clanks against the crystal. "Maybe."

"You're wise," I say. "What do you think's going on?"

"If by wise you mean that I'm old and I've been around"—she pulls out the copper spoon and jabs it in my direction—"you're exactly right."

She places the spoon on a towel and gestures to the silver tray and four martini glasses on the small built-in wet bar behind me.

I carefully lift the tray and place it in front of her. She uses a strainer to pour two drinks, leaving the other two empty, since Lily texted that she and Alec were caught in traffic and would be a few minutes late.

May skewers olives with silver Samurai sword–shaped cocktail picks she purchased from Bubbles & More and drops one into each glass. She hands me one, and we lift the cocktails in a silent cheers.

"What do I think?" she says before taking a sip of her martini and leaving a coral lipstick mark behind. "I think they've forgotten how to be in love. And I think you have more important things to worry about."

"Like the store," I say, sipping my drink.

"Sugar, no. I mean, yes, you've got your work cut out for you there. But what you have no business fretting over is your sister's love life. At least she has one."

"Um, ouch."

"Oh, tits up," she says. "Now, tell me who's got you smiling at your phone all the time."

"I do *not* smile at my phone."

She takes a long sip and stares me down, and because I've *never* been able to weather that particular look, I relent.

"Okay," I take a drink. "There's sort of a guy. Who I haven't met. And could be a pervert."

I've told enough people about Sir now to brace for the usual warnings, but sometimes even I forget that May is May and has her own rule book.

"Oh, you've got yourself an Alfred Kralik."

"A who now?"

"A very handsome James Stewart writing very romantic letters to a very beautiful Margaret Sullivan. Do your homework, but do it later. Tell me about your man. Have you seen his package yet?"

I choke on my martini. "May!"

"Clutch your pearls all you want, dick pics are common-place nowadays."

"In what world?"

"Hmm, either you haven't mustered up the courage to see the proof in the pudding or his thing's crooked."

"I'm not interested in his *thing*! We're just friends. He's a confidant."

"Honey, I'm a confidant. Your sister is a confidant. This is a *Situation*." She draws out each syllable of the word.

"It's . . . something," I admit.

"Oh yes," she says inhaling deeply. "I've had a couple ro-mantic pen pals myself."

"Really?" I lean forward, always marveling that I've known May most of my life, yet I feel like I'm nowhere close to un-covering all her secrets.

"Mm-hmm. One during Vietnam, though he went home and married some proper girl and moved to Jersey." She gives me a thumbs down and makes a splat noise. "Another was from San Francisco. This was when I was in my late teens. His letter was meant for Janet next door—horrid girl. They'd met at summer camp. He seemed too good for her, so I wrote him back, and he became my pen pal instead."

"What happened?" I slide the olive off its pick with my teeth.

"He died. Boating accident."

I blink. "Neither of those are good stories, May."

"Sure they are. Just not happy ones. Because here's the thing, young lady. Those sort of long-distance flirtations are all well and good, they're memorable, but they aren't the real deal. And if you've started telling yourself this is the real deal, it's time to nip that in the bud, because that's a fantasy. And fantasies do not warm the bed at night, nor do they help shoulder the burden of what's going on with your business right now— Oh shit! I forgot to take the foil off the lasagna."

May pulls on hot mitts that look like shark heads and tends to her eggplant lasagna.

I sigh. She's right. And I don't love that she's right. This thing with Sir isn't out of control, so to speak, but I'm no longer sure it's harmless. I spend a little too much time thinking about him. I'm starting to wonder if it's closed me off to looking at other men. I've gotten a handful of invitations to meet from other guys on the MysteryMate app, but they all seem so flat compared to him.

Other than customers and the vile Sebastian Andrews, I can't even remember the last meaningful conversation I've had with a man.

I'm saved from my own thoughts by the old-fashioned buzzer connected to the doorman downstairs.

"Let your sister and brother up," May orders as she begins mixing the second batch of martinis for the latecomers.

I do as she says, and a couple of minutes after I tell John downstairs to let them up, I'm opening May's front door to Lily and Alec. Lily's dressed as impeccably as ever in skinny black jeans and a cute twisty top with bows at the shoulder.

Though she smiles, there are circles under her eyes. I squeeze her extra tight before turning toward Alec.

My brother-in-law's a good-looking guy. Not particularly tall, but he's religious about his daily workouts, and his lack of height is made up for with broad shoulders, a quietly commanding presence, and kind brown eyes.

I extend a hand. "Hi, I'm Gracie. You look sort of familiar, but I can't put my finger on how I know you . . ."

He rolls his eyes and hauls me in for a hug. "I know I've been a little absent lately, message received loud and clear."

I hug him extra tight too, because I sense he needs it as much as Lily does. When I pull back and look at the two of them, my heart sinks as I realize there really is a stiffness between them.

May bustles into the room with her tray of martinis, bacon appetizers, and mixed nuts and orders everyone to sit. We've been to May's dozens of time over the years, and we each have our spots. Caleb and I on the long floral couch next to my dad, Lily and Alec on the matching love seat, and May in what she calls her throne, an ugly brown wing chair.

Tonight, Lily sits beside me on the couch.

I want to believe it's because she doesn't want to remind me that Dad's gone and Caleb's in another state, and I'm sure that's partially it. But the way she carefully avoids looking at Alec when he sits on the love seat—alone—makes me think there's more to it.

May's eyes narrow, telling me she sees it too, but for once, she seems to decide to bite her tongue.

"So, Gracie," Alec says, leaning forward and grabbing a handful of nuts. "I hear you guys have some new ideas for the store?"

"Yes!" I gush in my best cheerful, middle-child, smooth-the-waters tone. "We're starting off with a champagne tasting next Thursday. Robyn's convinced one of her sommelier friends who has a New York food blog to cover it. We've got reps from two different wineries hosting tables, and one of my friends just started dating a jazz pianist who's going to bring his trio for some live music."

Alec smiles. "Sounds amazing."

"It will be," I say confidently. "You should come."

"He can't," Lily interjects, not looking up from the bacon-wrapped ricotta she's studying intently. "He's traveling. Again."

Nervously, I glance back at Alec, expecting to see irritation or anger at his wife's thinly veiled feelings about his schedule. Instead, he's staring at Lily with a look of longing and dismay that is so raw I feel a lump in my throat.

Lily, still studying her appetizer, sees none of this.

When her blue eyes do finally sneak over to him, he's reaching for his martini, his expression shut down.

On second thought, maybe I'll cling to my online fantasy just a little bit longer. It looks a lot less painful than this.

Ten

"I love so much that you're here," I wrap my arm around Lily's shoulders and kiss her cheek.

She smiles. "I should have been here long before this. It was unfair of Caleb and me to let this all rest on your shoulders. I'm sorry."

"Forgiven," I say, in too good a mood to even think about holding a grudge.

Lily has been setting out the rented champagne flutes, and wordlessly we begin working together, her taking them out of the plastic crate, me setting them on the table.

The theme for the tasting party tonight is *la reentrée*, a French term for the return to "real life" after the summer holiday. Considering it's early October, we're a little late for the theme, but since the summer humidity's just now relented, everyone seems to be in a cheerful *welcome fall!* mood this week.

Everyone except my sister, who despite dutifully helping with whatever I've asked, hasn't made a single comment on the pretty glass-blown pumpkins or the glittery fall leaves on the table, and she normally *loves* all things autumn.

"Plus," she says distractedly, "it's nice to have something to keep me busy."

I reach out and begin lining the glasses into tidy rows. "Where's Alec again?"

"Chicago. Oh wait, no. Boston? I can't remember." Her voice is completely checked out, as though she really doesn't know when he gets back and doesn't care one way or the other.

"Any fun plans for the weekend?" I ask, trying to get a little spark out of her.

"Not really. I've got a few things to do around the house."

"You and Alec should go somewhere," I say casually, continuing to straighten the glasses. "What about the Hamptons? Off-season you shouldn't have trouble finding a place. Or even just a day trip up to the Hudson Valley to one of the farmer's markets?"

She stops pulling glasses out, and there's genuine confusion on her face, as though I've just suggested she shave her head or take up needlework.

I think about May's assessment: *they've forgotten how to be in love.*

I'm afraid she's right, and I have no idea what to do about it. I probably shouldn't do anything about it. It's not my relationship, and it's not my business.

Yet when I think of Lily and Alec, I don't see them as they've been recently—tired. Tense. I see them on their prom night. The morning after they'd gotten engaged. Their wedding day. The day they bought their place.

I believe in my very core that theirs is a happily-ever-after ending. They've just hit the poison-apple stage of their story.

She looks down and reaches for the base of another glass, and I gently touch the back of her hand. "Lil, what's going on?"

I hear her swallow, then see her long eyelashes bat repeatedly against her cheeks, and I know she's blinking away tears.

"We have faulty junk," she says on a watery voice.

I let out a startled laugh. "What?"

She discreetly uses her sleeve to dab at her nose. "IVF didn't take. The fertility specialist told us a couple months ago that while it wasn't impossible for us to conceive, we may want to consider alternative methods of starting a family."

"Oh, Lily." I immediately move to hug her, but she gives a quick shake of her head. I know she's trying desperately to hold it together, so instead I squeeze her arm.

"I thought I'd made peace with it. We talked about a surrogate, adoption, but then we just sort of . . . stopped talking."

"Why, do you think?"

She squeezes her eyes shut. "I'm so mad at him. I wanted to start a family years ago, but he kept saying he wanted to build his career first. At the time, I loved him all the more for it. Both because he wanted to make sure he could support me and a baby, and because he said he wanted to put in the long hours *then* so that when we started a family, he could be the sort of dad who was around. And of course, you always hear that women's fertility decreases as they age, but I just . . . I really thought it would happen for us."

"Maybe it still can. Or like you said, there are other ways to become a mom, and you'd make such a great one."

"I know," she says with such Lily-like confidence I smile in spite of the heartache I feel for my sister—and for Alec too.

"Have you guys thought about therapy?"

She snorts. "He'd have to actually be around for that. I've been distant—I'll admit that. But his way of dealing with it is to work more than ever. Now we hardly see each other, and when we do, there's just this . . . distance."

Lily sighs. "I don't know what to do, Gracie. I genuinely don't. Maybe you're the smart one, steering clear of men. Why do they have to be so *difficult*?"

For some reason, my first thought is Sebastian Andrews. Difficult doesn't begin to explain the man. Or what I feel when I'm around him.

To say nothing of the mysterious Sir.

Both of whom are taken.

Difficult indeed.

"You know I'm here. If you want to talk," I say softly.

"I know," she says, pulling me in for a hug. "I forget sometimes that my little sister no longer needs my help to put her hair in a bun for ballet class and can actually be a pretty good listener."

We wrap our arms around each other, and I squeeze her tight. "What are the chances you could help me with my hair just one more time?"

She pulls back and gives me a critical once-over that doesn't bother me as much as it usually might, because it means that for now, at least, her attention is on something other than her heartache. "You're not wearing that, right?"

I do a sexy sway in my frumpy clothes and tennis shoes. "Of course I am. A journalist is covering the tasting tonight.

What if they want my picture to go with the article? I must look my best!"

She shakes her head, and I push her to the back of the store and into the small staff bathroom, pulling the garment bag off the small hook on the door. I hear her turn on the small space heater, then unzip the bag and let out an un-Lily-like squeal, "Oh, I *love* this dress! I haven't seen you wear it in forever."

"I rediscovered it the other day," I say as she takes the dress off the hanger and hands it to me. It's the same blue dress I wore to Sebastian's office, and even though that meeting didn't quite go as planned, I'd liked the way I felt when I wore it.

Plus, if I'm honest, my closet is sort of slim pickings since my wardrobe budget really only has room for underwear and bulk buys of men's undershirts.

"Please tell me you brought something to fix your hair too," she says as I change, rummaging through the free tote bag I got from a book fair in Brooklyn. "Aha!" she says in triumph, pulling out a curling iron and plugging it in.

I slip on tan flats with a leather bow across the toe—no chance the pink heels would have made it all night.

Lily pulls the elastic out of my hair, freeing it from its limp ponytail, and then begins winding sections of my hair around the wide barrel, twisting each strand in a different direction than the last to avoid what she informs me would be "Shirley Temple curls."

"Where's your hairspray?" she demands.

"Um . . ."

She sighs. "Without it, these curls won't last more than an hour, but it's better than the pony. I guess."

"Stop with the effusive compliments. I'm getting embarrassed!"

"Stay," she says, holding up a finger in command.

A moment later she returns with a folding chair and her own purse and pulls out a makeup bag. She opens the chair and points. "Let me fix your face."

"I didn't realize it needed fixing," I grumble, but I sit.

"It doesn't," she says, adding bronzer to my temples. "You're perfect. But tonight, we need to take all the girl-next-door cuteness and channel woman-next-door success. Turn." She twirls her finger, and I turn to the mirror.

"Wow! Not bad! You've come a long way since the blue eye shadow and red blush of my recital days," I say.

"Hey, I stand by that look," Lily says. She lifts one of my curls and moves it to the other side of my head. "There. Now it has some more body." She smiles. "You look beautiful, and I am a genius."

I roll my eyes and check my watch. "Oh crap! People are already arriving!"

"May's got it," she says soothingly. "Tonight's going to be really great. I know Dad used to do the occasional tasting, but not like this, not at night, with live music and super cute pumpkin decorations."

"You *did* notice them!" I say, delighted. "I knew you'd love those. Let's just hope everyone else does. Actually, I just hope they show up."

The nervousness I'd been carefully avoiding hits me all at once, because despite the fact that I'd handed out flyers to my fellow local businesses, called every friend I've ever made, and posted the event on social media, I have no idea if people will show.

Lily holds my hand as I open the door to the cave, and immediately the nervousness dissipates into happiness. The event only started ten minutes ago, and while it's not exactly a packed house, there are enough people milling around to make it feel like an actual party.

I smile as I look around. The band is seriously *good*, and people—even Robyn—are smiling, the vendors sponsoring the tasting have an engaged audience, May seems delighted by the man delighted by her amply displayed cleavage, and . . .

Across the room, a pretty freckled blonde in a pristine white dress listens with rapt attention as the vendor from a Napa winery explains the nuances of her blanc de blanc. Her male companion isn't paying attention at all.

He's too busy glaring at me, and when his aqua eyes lock with mine, he lifts his glass in a silent, mocking toast.

Though we don't exchange a single word, by silent agreement, Sebastian Andrews and I find ourselves alone in a secluded corner of the shop where we can bicker in private. The art corner. *My* art corner, not that I'll ever let him in on that little fact.

He's holding two glasses, and I'm thrown off guard when he hands one to me. I blink in surprise, and he shrugs. "It's from the California label. A blanc de pinot noir."

It rolls off his tongue, the way it would for someone effortlessly familiar with sparkling wine, not someone who'd just learned the term at a tasting. Another surprise. Irritating.

"What are you doing here?" I ask.

"Oh, I'm sorry," he says, clearly not the least bit sorry. "Was it invitation only?"

"No, but—"

His head dips forward so he can speak softly into my ear. "Maybe I just like to support small local businesses."

I try to come up with a witty response, but his closeness is annoyingly distracting.

When he pulls back and meets my eyes, there's a slight playfulness to his expression I've never seen before. Along with last week's revelation about Avis and Jesse, and his clear affection for his parents, the man is turning out to have layers.

A development that is highly annoying.

His eyes move away from mine, slowly, almost reluctantly, as he seems to realize where we are. His gaze flits from painting to painting. "Fairies."

"Cutesy Tinker Bell," I correct. Then, because I can't help but want to defend my range as an artist, I point out, "And they're not all fairies."

"No, they're not. This one in particular is clever." He points his glass to the purple cocktail with a whimsical violet Manhattan skyline in the background. I'd added it just this afternoon after working around the clock trying to get it done in time for this party in hopes it would find a new home.

"Genevieve would love it," he adds. "Purple's her favorite color."

My usually full-flavored blanc de pinot noir, with notes of strawberries and cherry, suddenly tastes sour.

"You should get it for her," I say mildly, turning so we're standing shoulder to shoulder. "Better yet, let me get it for you. It would make a fabulous engagement gift."

I say it to needle him, a reminder that I'd overheard his conversation with his marriage-minded mother.

But I feel a little guilty about it when I see a troubled look cross his face.

"I'm sorry," I say quietly. "That's really none of my business."

"No, it's not." Then he looks down at his glass. "It's complicated."

"How so?" I ask, because I'm genuinely curious, especially now I know his and Genevieve's intertwined history. Even more bafflingly though, I want to know because it seems he actually wants to tell me.

"Well, for starters, we're not dating."

My head whips around. "What?"

He lifts a shoulder and looks back at the watercolor, but I don't sense he's really seeing it. "We're just friends. We have been our entire life, though my mother wasn't wrong about our dating history. We've dated on and off since we were teens, trying to make it work because it feels like it should work. Up until a few months ago we were on again, but I called it." He pauses. "This time for good."

I blink. "But you guys still came together tonight?"

He gives a small half smile. "She loves champagne. And when you're as well practiced at breaking up as Gen and me, and still have to see each other at holidays, you get pretty good at going straight to the friends stage with minimal awkwardness."

"That's impressive," I murmur. "Why for good this time on the breakup?"

He says nothing.

"Hmm, okay, stop me when I get close," I say, taking a sip of wine. We both pretend to study the art as I begin rattling off the potential snags to their relationship. "You're gay. She's gay. She likes cats. You're a dog person. Opposing political views. One of you likes pineapple on your pizza, and the other thinks fruit on pizza's an aberration. She wants to summer in East Hampton, you in Southampton. You have a porn addiction. You have different tastes in china patterns. She falls asleep to whale noises, but you like silence and a night-light. There's someone else—"

His eyes flick over to me, just for a second, but it's unmistakably a tell.

"Ah," I say lightly, trying to ignore the way my heart irrationally soars at the realization he's single, only to tumble again at the realization that there's another woman in the picture. "Tricky."

"It's not like that," he says a little irritably.

I look up at him questioningly.

"It's just . . ." He exhales with a quiet laugh. "Complicated. And I don't know why I'm telling you this."

"Maybe because you know I already think you're the worst, and thus you can tell me anything without my opinion of you sinking any lower?" I say, batting my eyelashes.

He rolls his eyes, then turns to face me. "What about you?" he asks, glancing my way. "In a relationship?"

"Sort of," I say, thinking of Sir. Then I smile and echo his words. "It's complicated."

For a moment, I think he might smile back, and it feels like we understand each other in a way I haven't felt understood in a really long time. Well, outside of my online conversations with Sir.

Is it just me? I want to know.

"What?" he prods, as though sensing the question I haven't voiced.

I take a tiny sip of my champagne for courage and decide to feel brave. "That day we first met. Did you—" My courage fades slightly, and I press my lips together and look down at my shoes as I try again. "Did you feel . . ."

His gaze sharpens. "What? Did I feel what?"

I swallow, and when May barks my name in her sharp drill sergeant voice, I jump. I lose my nerve. I start to turn to see what she wants, but Sebastian's gaze holds me frozen, silently trying to tell me something . . .

"Gracie?" May says again, gentler this time.

Reluctantly, I turn and see May and Robyn standing beside a lanky man with a large nose, who I know from Twitter is the sommelier blogger I need to woo if I want a good write-up for the shop.

I have never resented my obligation to Bubbles & More as much as I do in this moment, but as always, I do what needs to be done.

I take a deep breath and step away from Sebastian. "Please excuse me."

He nods, and I feel his eyes on my back as I walk away.

We don't speak the rest of the evening, and yet every time I search the room for him, which is admittedly often, he's standing by Genevieve's side, nodding pleasantly at whomever he's speaking to.

And every time, he seems to sense my gaze, because his eyes find mine. The moments of eye contact are brief—a few seconds at most.

The butterflies in my stomach last much, much longer.

To Sir, with aggravation,

Do you ever want something you can't have—that you shouldn't want? But the more you try to stop, the harder you want?

Lady

———————

My dear Lady,

Very much so. And I hope you get what you want that you can't have—at least one of us should.

Yours in yearning,

Sir

———————

To Sir,

What is it you yearn for?

Lady

Eleven

Sir doesn't reply to my last message, but I can't stop thinking about his.

Yours *in yearning*.

Yearning!

My thoughts of Sebastian haven't faded, but now they're competing with thoughts of Sir, each man as unattainable as the other, and each causing twin pulls of, well, *yearning*.

After three straight days of what I can only describe as teenage pining after the champagne tasting and Sir's last message, I get sick of my mopey self and throw myself into my art with a vengeance in a desperate attempt to forget about both men.

I don't remember when I first fell in love with art. It's just always been a part of my life, the thing I was meant to do. Finger paints. Construction paper. Pastels. I loved it all, and I was good at it all.

Or as much a master of finger paints as anyone can be.

And my love for art only increased with each passing year. In eighth grade, a student from a local art school had come in to teach us how to sketch a still life. Most of the kids had been glad that the art lesson had replaced social studies for the day.

But man, I was really into that bowl of fruit. I erased the shading on the apple so many times that the art student—Juliet—had had to get me a new sheet of paper, and she'd stayed with me after school awhile longer to explain how changing the angle of how I held the pencil could help create dimension in my strokes.

Most vividly of all though, I remember when I realized watercolors were my *thing*. It was a Sunday afternoon. I was seventeen, and Caleb and I had spent the morning helping my dad dust all of the bottles before the shop opened at noon. The rest of the day was ours, since he'd hired May by that point.

We were heading home through Central Park—a route I was allowed to take only during the day, and only when the younger but much larger Caleb was with me. Caleb had been going through a nerdy but intense Ultimate Frisbee stage, and when he'd spotted a pickup game on one of the lawns, had begged to play for a few minutes.

Since I was behind on my summer reading, I settled on a bench with the intent to make progress on *The Grapes of Wrath*, but Steinbeck couldn't hold a candle to the art class happening a few feet away.

A group of ten adults stood in front of one of Central Park's iconic bridges, as a wiry man with a big bushy beard wound around them, offering blunt pointers and gruff words of encouragement.

I was familiar with watercolors as a medium, but my actual experience was limited to one day in fifth grade. The paint quality had been crap, the brushes may as well have been pieces of straw, and the paper was regular old computer paper.

Needless to say, I didn't understand the full magic of watercolors.

But from my place on the bench that day, I was fascinated by how the same subject could look so different from one artist to the next. As I crept closer, I could see the unpredictable way the colors blended, or didn't blend. The way those who were generous with their water had a soft wash of pastel color and those who were more reserved had a more vivid result.

An irritable woman wearing an actual beret had loudly, and passive aggressively, mentioned that she'd thought the class was forty dollars while giving me the side-eye.

Embarrassed, I'd pulled out the blue Fossil wallet Dad got me for Christmas. The crusty instructor had looked down at my two fives and two ones—all of my allowance—and instead of pointing out that I was twenty-eight short, had refused my cash with a wink, and instead handed me his own paints and brush to use for the afternoon.

Another, much nicer woman than the first had given me an extra pad and a pop-up easel, which she'd brought for a friend who couldn't make it.

I'm not going to tell you my painting of the bridge that day was better than anyone else's—it was an intermediate class, and I was a definite beginner—but it hadn't mattered. It wasn't the bridge that had called to me, it was the medium. Watching the class paint in watercolors paled in comparison to experimenting myself.

By the time I looked up, my bridge was largely a blur of

color, thanks to one too many trial and errors, and most of the class had dispersed. My eyes had watered when I'd given the paints back to the instructor because I knew he'd given me something far more longer lasting than his paints, which I later learned were professional quality and very expensive.

Caleb's Frisbee game had ended, and though I'm sure sitting and watching a bunch of amateurs paint was the last thing a restless fifteen-year-old boy had wanted to do with his afternoon, I think his sibling intuition had kicked in and he knew dragging me home would have been cruel.

On our walk home, he'd told me that I'd looked possessed "and a little psycho."

The next afternoon, I was sitting on the couch suffering through Steinbeck when Caleb came home from a friend's house and unceremoniously dumped a plastic bag into my lap. Without a word, he headed into the bathroom, and I upended the bag.

My brother had bought me a set of watercolors, blue plastic brushes, and a sketchbook filled with thick paper. The supplies weren't fancy, but I also knew he'd been carefully saving up his allowance to buy a new video game—and he'd spent it on these art supplies instead.

I'd cried and hugged him until he'd threatened to return everything if I didn't stop. I've never loved my brother more.

My dad was another story. He wasn't *un*supportive—any art supplies I put on my Christmas lists over the years were generally found under the tree—but my "craft time" always had to come after homework (fair) and my duties at Bubbles (at times, that felt less fair).

My dad was a real follow-your-passion type of guy. As long as it was *his* passion. By the time Lily had married and more or less moved on from the shop, Caleb kept himself busy with girls, sports, and school, working at Bubbles only on the occasional weekend. I was busy too. I had friends. The occasional boyfriend. Classes. But none of this had stopped my dad from assuming I'd be available to work at the shop when he asked, and I felt too guilty about abandoning him to say no.

I can't pretend teenage me didn't occasionally resent that Caleb could be off doing whatever he wanted, that Lily had escaped by way of Alec, and that I was stuck at the store. But I also *liked* that Dad called me his right-hand woman. I liked that I eventually knew the store even better than know-it-all Lily. I liked that I was May's favorite, and probably Dad's too.

But what I liked more than *any* of that were the afternoons and rare days off when I could just paint.

Days like today, when Robyn and Josh are manning the store on what is likely to be a quiet Tuesday, as most Tuesdays are. Days where the only thing on my to-do list is to clean out that funky Tupperware in the fridge (I'll get to it) and work on my latest painting.

I'm loving this one. It's got sharper edges than usual. A rocks glass. Amber liquid—whisky, I guess, though I don't drink it. The background, as with most of my work, is New York, but it's New York seen through the panes of a window— an apartment window. A man's apartment window.

I've painted men before, but usually as part of a couple— strolling through Central Park holding hands, a bottle of champagne in his free hand, two flutes in hers. And I've done a few bride and groom pieces on request and a Valentine's series that sold out almost immediately.

But this is the first time I've done a man alone. I don't know that it'll sell—my clientele is almost entirely female, or men buying for women. But I'm enjoying the challenge of trying to convey Clooney-level attractiveness, a touch of Dean Martin charm, with Clint Eastwood's gravitas.

I put on my headphones, turn on Queen, and lose myself in "Bohemian Rhapsody."

An hour later, when my hand cramps and my playlist runs out, there's a woman in my kitchen who was not there when I started.

My heart jumps but settles quickly. I've grown used to Keva letting herself in, and without my ever having to tell her, she's always known not to interrupt me when I'm working. Often, it's the smells that pull me out of the zone, and I'm wondering how I didn't notice before now, because my apartment smells like brown-buttery heaven.

"Hey, babe," she says over her shoulder, fussing with something on the stove with one hand, pouring herself a glass of wine with the other. She lifts the bottle. "Chianti?"

"Why not?" I get myself a glass, and she pours without spilling a drop, even though her gaze never leaves the grilled cheese.

I look around my kitchen. There is *a lot* of grilled cheese, with about a half dozen different breads and cheeses.

"PMS craving?"

"Not entirely a bad guess," she says, using the edge of a spatula—hers, not mine, she hates my kitchen tools—to test the crispness of what looks to be raisin bread.

"Last-minute baby shower tomorrow. Some local politician's wife has apparently been craving grilled cheese for her entire pregnancy, so they're going with a grilled cheese bar and want six different options. I talked them down from ten, which is just nuts. And since Grady's got a date tonight, I'm on my own to come up with the selections, which suits me fine since he had the gall to suggest *cashew* cheese."

"Horror," I say loyally, scanning the half dozen sandwiches on my counters. "Are any of these rejects?"

"Take your pick and be honest about your thoughts, because they're all good, and I've got to narrow it down. But don't even think about axing the smoked Gouda on sourdough, browned in bacon fat. That stays. Oh, and imagine all of them infinitely better, because they'll be made with homemade bread, which is rising upstairs. Hence why I'm here." She waggles the spatula at me. "The temperature upstairs is *just* right for bread rising, and I can't mess with it."

The sandwiches all sort of look the same, so I pick up the one closest to me and take a bite of the corner, my eyes closing as I let out a low moan. The cheese is creamy and a tiny bit funky, and there's both a sweetness and a bitterness that play off each other perfectly.

"Taleggio, escarole, and caramelized onions," she says, pushing her headband back with her wine hand.

"I normally wouldn't let a leafy green near my grilled

cheese," I say, wiping my mouth with the back of my hand. "But the bitterness really works here. This makes the short list."

I pick up another sandwich that looks a lot like the grilled cheese we used to get on Fridays in school, only a million times better. I stare at the sandwich in wonder. "I don't remember American cheese tasting like this."

"That's because it's homemade," she says.

"Please, let's run away together." I take another bite, wash it down with wine, and stare at my friend adoringly. "Live happily ever after, just us and this cheese."

"I totally would," she says, checking the underside of the sandwich she's making and then flipping off the burner. "But you're missing a body part I *really* like. Though, if I keep having dates like last night, don't think I won't come knocking."

"I thought you were excited about this one." I ponder my other sandwich options and pick up one with apples and Brie, I think.

"I was. He told me I looked like Beyoncé."

"So?" I say around a delicious mouthful. "That's a major compliment."

"Girl, anytime a man tells you that you look like Queen Bey on the first date, before the bruschetta even gets to the table and while ogling your boobs, he's looking for one night and one night only. *Bleck*," she says, holding her palms up. "Not even worth discussion."

She picks up one of the grilled cheeses I've already tried, adds her own bite mark, then gestures toward my work in progress with the sandwich. "You seemed super into it today—didn't even notice when I got distracted grating cheese and burned the butter on round two."

I roll my shoulders a little and wipe my greasy fingers on my dirty painting smock. "Yeah, trying something a little different. Masculine. A little cooler. Hard to get the lines right. It started out too washed out, then got too dark, but after a few false starts, I'm happy with it."

"I love it. It's enchanting, as your stuff always is, but it's a little sexy too. Plus, the eyes on that guy." She gives a sexy shiver. "Can you imagine if they made eyes that color in real life? You'd have to hose me down on the regular."

The eyes? I frown and glance over at my painting, then toss the sandwich I've just picked up back onto the plate, appetite gone.

I've made the man's eyes aqua.

So much for my art helping me forget about men.

To Sir, in shameless prying,

I know you ended up on this app as a mistake, but I've found myself wondering—why did your friend set up a profile for you on THIS app? It's hardly the most popular—and the idea of being matched with someone you've never seen is not everyone's cup of tea.

Lady

My dear Lady,

Fair question. At the bachelor party in question, the groom and his fiancée had met on this very dating app. And I hope I don't cause offense here, but I expressed blunt disbelief that this method of courtship could be effective. I was too much of a traditionalist to believe in falling in love over the Internet, much less with a person whose face I've never seen.

I believe the creation of this account without my knowledge was in direct retaliation to my blunt skepticism.

Yours in curiosity, hopefully abated,

Sir

———

To Sir,

No offense taken, though I would have to note that this is one area where you and I will not agree. I too am a traditionalist, which is why I would argue that there's something lovely about two souls connecting over words alone. Though, that being said, it could be argued that you have the stronger case, actually being in a relationship with someone you met in person, whereas I haven't had any luck finding love on this blasted thing.

Lady

_____

My dear Lady,

Not so much as an advantage as you may think. The relationship you reference has run its course. And the fact that you haven't had any luck finding love, well, I'll confess to finding that regrettable.

Sir

twelve

My love life may be a hot mess, but professionally, things have never been better. Or more hectic. In the weeks following the champagne tasting (which Robyn's blogger friend had described as "a welcome touch of old-world charm"), I've launched a weekly raffle where customers can drop off a business card or jot their name and number down for a chance to win a gift basket.

We've had a *guess that grape* happy hour, where we open a bottle of something fun and let people try to identify the grapes in exchange for little gift items.

Even Robyn's gotten into the innovative spirit and is taking the lead on a champagne trivia night. But it's Lily's original idea, a cooking class, that has required the most planning, and that I'm most excited about.

We decided to cater to couples for the first version in the hopes that there's a market for fresh date-night ideas. There's no chance I could have pulled it off if I didn't happen to have a best friend and neighbor who works at a catering company. Without Keva and Grady graciously lending me some of their equipment—for free—and donating their time, also for free, I'm pretty sure it would be a financial loss.

Instead, the only things Bubbles is paying for outright are employees—May, Josh, and Robyn are all working tonight—and the grocery bill, which may I just say is . . . *not cheap*.

But then, neither were the tickets. Which worried me at first. In order to cover the food and the champagne *and* make a profit, I'd had to charge three hundred per couple.

May's been managing the reservations, and not only did we fill all twelve seats, but there was a wait list of people asking to be called if there were any cancellations, which so far there haven't been.

It feels a bit like a miracle, though not as much a miracle as the fact that Keva and Robyn, two people who strike me as oil and water, have become instafriends over the process of planning the menu and wine pairings.

Ten minutes before the class is set to begin, I'm checking to make sure all the stations have the right glassware when I glance over to see Keva with something in her hand, going for Robyn's face.

"Oh, I don't think so," Robyn is saying, shaking her head rapidly as she grabs Keva's wrist. "Gracie, tell her I can't pull that off."

Closer now, I can see the object in hand: Keva's trademark Dior red lip lacquer.

"Tell her she has to wear it," Keva insists. "I can't take one more minute of looking at that dead brown."

"It's matte black cherry," Robyn says stubbornly, defending her own signature lip look.

"It's terrible," Keva insists. "Gracie, tell her."

I will do no such thing, though I agree that Robyn's black cherry isn't exactly a look I can get excited about.

"Keva, leave her alone. Also, I've been begging you to let *me* try your lip color, and you're forcing it on her?"

"Honey, no. This is all wrong for you," Keva tells me, still focused on Robyn's mouth as though plotting how to sneak attack her.

Robyn nods in agreement. "Definitely all wrong. It'd wash you out."

"Really?" I ask her. "I just defended you against Keva's lipstick bullying."

"Just try it," Keva says, her attention still on Robyn. "If you hate it, I've got makeup remover wipes in my purse and you can go back to looking like a corpse from the nineties."

A skeptical-looking Robyn narrows her eyes on the sleek black tube, then sighs and holds out her hand. "Fine."

"No, no." Keva bats her hand away and steps forward, grabbing Robyn's chin and forcing her mouth into a pucker. She applies the red lacquer and steps back.

I blink. In the span of ten seconds, Robyn looks like an entirely different person.

Keva tilts her head. "What do we think, Gracie? It's a little orange, but I'm into it."

"You look . . ." *Alive. Friendly. Nice.* "It looks really good on you," I tell Robyn.

She looks doubtful, and when she opens the compact Keva hands her to inspect her look, her expression betrays nothing. She snaps the compact shut and hands it back. "I like it."

"I know," Keva says with a shrug.

"*So* glad that's sorted," I say. "Now about the fact that we have twelve people arriving any minute—"

"Uh-uh." Keva lifts a finger. "Remember what I told you? No fussing. I've taught dozens of cooking classes, so a simple three-course meal is no biggie. And Rob's got the wine notes covered. The English sparkling wine she's paired with the crab cakes is going to blow your mind. Now"—she waggles her fingers in dismissal—"I have to practice my opener."

"You have an opener?"

"I'm an entertainer."

Robyn nods in solidarity, and I shake my head, unsure if I'm annoyed or delighted by their alliance.

The couples start to trickle in, quiet and a little unsure at first, but the noise level slowly rises as the welcome sparkling wine Robyn's selected begins to work its magic and couples claim their stations.

The supplies may have been loaned for free, but setup hadn't exactly been a breeze. In order to make room for six wheeled chef counters topped with induction burners and cutting boards, we'd had to move several racks, and some of our floor inventory had to be placed temporarily in the cave. Still, Bubbles is good-sized for a Manhattan brick and mortar, so with a little creativity, not only did we get all six stations to fit, we were also able to space them out so each couple would have their own little section.

It's a pretty fantastic date night, if I do say so myself. Not that I can, because I haven't had one in forever.

Also? Sir is single.

I repeat. Sir. Is. Single.

I'm torn between elation and disappointment that he hasn't expressed any interest in meeting, or transitioning our relationship from whatever we are to something a little more intimate.

Then there's also the annoying fact that I'm a tiny bit relieved, because I can't seem to get a certain aqua-eyed businessman out of my head.

"All good?" I ask May, who's been handling check-in on the store's iPad. Her earrings are shaped like gummy worms tonight, one red and yellow, the other green and yellow.

"All good. Though, station six is a half show," she says, pointing in the direction of the art corner. My watercolors are always carefully wrapped in plastic, but I'd moved them all out of reach to the upper shelves tonight, just in case.

"A half show?" I ask.

"Only half the couple showed up."

"Oh." My heart twinges a little for the solo person. "That's a little . . . sad."

"Exactly," she says ushering me forward. "Which is why he needs a partner."

"No way," I say, trying to dig in my heels, but May's built like a bull, and the poor single male is the red flag being waved in front of her.

"It can't be me. I've got to oversee—"

"Nonsense. Your girl Keva is in charge, Robyn's second-in-command, you've got me and Josh here to take care of the unexpected, and Lily's on call. If we need you, you'll know."

She maneuvers me to the table, picks up the plain black

apron Keva had provided, and thrusts it at me. "Have fun," she says with a wink.

Sighing, I turn to apologize to the paying customer who I'm pretty sure has no interest in cooking alongside the shop owner all night.

He turns to face me, and all seems just a little bit more right in the world.

Sebastian's face betrays nothing as he looks down at me. "Ms. Cooper."

"Mr. Andrews." I swallow. "Where's your date? Is your mystery woman meeting you here tonight?"

I'm more than a little curious about the mysterious, *complicated* woman responsible for him ending things with Genevieve.

He lifts his shoulders. "I'm solo tonight."

I wait for him to elaborate, and when he doesn't, I narrow my eyes. "Mr. Andrews. What are you doing here?"

"Learning what sort of food pairs with champagne."

My eyes narrow further. "First the champagne party. Now this. You're *spying* on me. Hoping I'll fail, so you can swoop in with your offer the second I do."

"Yes," he says mildly. "Spending three hundred dollars tonight is a stellar example of monetary sabotage."

Josh appears, carrying a tray of flutes filled with the welcome wine. We're apparently Josh's last stop, because there are only two glasses on his carefully balanced tray—he'd spent all afternoon practicing with plastic cups filled with water—and Sebastian takes both of them, handing me one before I can protest.

"It's a German Riesling Sekt." Josh carefully enunciates the word that was unfamiliar to him until Robyn's coaching yesterday. "A fun, spirited sparkling wine with relatively low alcohol, a Bosc pear greeting, and a creamy vanilla finish that is requisite."

I carefully hide a smile at his perfect recitation of Robyn's note card. "Thank you, Josh." I start to hand him back the glass, but my shy employee is already rushing back to May.

Sebastian takes a sip. "It's good."

"Of course it's good. It's how we run a successful business."

I place just the slightest emphasis on successful to let him know that Bubbles & More is no closer to being bullied into closing.

Since the glass is in my hand, I take a small sip and study Sebastian, who seems strangely at ease for a single man in a room full of couples.

"Why not bring the other woman?" I ask.

"I'm sorry?"

"At the tasting you said you and Genevieve broke up because of someone else."

He glances down at the glass. "Is that what I said?"

"I—" *Wasn't it?* "Yes?"

"There's nobody here but you and me, Ms. Cooper."

As if I need the reminder. Every time I'm with the man, the rest of the world seems to fade away, and the Frank Sinatra songs in my head seem to be getting more and more intimate.

On the current playlist: "I'm a Fool to Want You"

Indeed, Frank. Indeed.

Thankfully, Keva's loud, booming voice takes command of

the room as she introduces herself and Robyn, as well as the structure of the class.

I don't want to interrupt or call attention to myself, so I move farther back into the corner, glancing over in surprise when Sebastian hooks the neck of the apron I set on the table on his index finger and holds it out to me, a clear challenge in his gaze.

I set my wine on the counter and snatch the black apron out of his hand, ignoring his smirk as I loop the thin tie over my head. I'm fumbling around for the back ties when I feel a hand brush mine. His hand.

I stand perfectly still as Sebastian ties a knot at my waist, his movements methodical and efficient. I turn my head to mutter an under-the-breath thank-you when his fingers drop to the side of my waist. My breath catches. His finger slips gently under the string—untwisting it, I realize—but then it stays just a moment longer than necessary. I feel his warmth, even through the fabric of my thin sweater, and I must have gulped my wine faster than I realized because I feel a little light-headed.

His hand slides away and he clears his throat slightly, picking up his flute once more and fixing all of his attention on Keva, who's explaining the first course—a smoked salmon blini, which she explains is a ten-dollar word for a tiny pancake, earning a laugh from the group—as Josh and May silently move around the room handing out baskets filled with all the necessary ingredients.

"Okay, for real. Why are you really here?" I ask Sebastian

once Keva's given us the instructions to get started. "Looking for a fire hazard? Violation of liquor license?"

"I like champagne, and I'd like to learn how to cook," he says, pulling a jar of capers out of our basket and studying it.

"You can't cook?"

"Not really. Can you?"

"No," I admit. "Well, sort of. Growing up, my brother, sister, and I all had to take care of dinner one night a week. My sister sometimes used an actual cookbook and put together something passably good, but my brother and I mostly embraced boxed pastas and jarred sauce."

"Did you have a specialty?" He hands me the package of smoked salmon.

"I make a pretty impressive Hamburger Helper, and my Chef Boyardee skills aren't bad either. You?"

"Delivery. I'm really, really good at ordering delivery," he replies.

I smile a little. I think maybe he does too.

Once our ingredients are laid out, Keva walks us through the next steps, encouraging those of us without a clear view of her table to come up for a closer look, which Sebastian and I do. She dices the red onion and salmon, grates a little lemon peel, mixes the blini batter . . . She makes it look easy.

Twenty minutes later, Sebastian looks over from the metal bowl he's stirring and inspects my cutting board. "It looks like you've just dissected something, and not very well."

"Yeah, well." I go on my toes to peer into his mixing bowl. "That looks like brain matter. Did hers have so many bubbles?"

Our eyes meet for a second. "Switch," we say at the same time as he hands me the bowl and moves behind me to take my place.

Ten laughing minutes after that, we sip the Deutz Millésime Robyn's selected and stand before the ultimate jury. Keva is standing in front of our counter, hands on hips, staring at our finished plate. She has yet to say a word.

Sebastian and I look at each other out of the corner of our eyes, and he rolls his lips inward as though to keep from laughing. I'm less successful, and a giggle bubbles out as I look again at what can only be described as a massacre. Somehow our pancake has managed to be both burned and completely raw, the salmon has been overworked to the point of looking like mush, and Sebastian got *way* too into grating the lemon, so there's a fine film of bright yellow covering the entire plate in a very neon-mold-type fashion.

Keva looks up and shakes her head at me. "How have you learned nothing from me over the years?"

"Okay, now hold on," I say, still trying not to laugh. "It doesn't *look* pretty, but it tastes good. You always say that it doesn't matter how food looks, as long as it's tasty."

"I'm a professional caterer. I have literally never said that," she says. "But you know what, go ahead and test that theory."

She hands us each a fork and lifts her eyebrows. Sebastian and I tentatively accept them. "You first," he says under his breath.

"Chicken," I mutter, and gingerly scoop a small bite onto my fork and lift it to my mouth.

"Oh God."

"Good?" he asks, taking a bite of his own. He makes one chewing motion then stops. "Oh God." He echoes.

I manage to chew and swallow the one bite, but I do not go for seconds, and neither does he. It's too salty from the capers (we added extra), weirdly crunchy from the lemon seed we accidentally got in there, and just all-around *way* too mushy.

Keva only shakes her head and walks away, looking bemused.

"We'll do better on the next one," I say, gulping water.

"We certainly can't do worse," he says, drinking his own water.

Robyn explains the next wine—the sparkling from England Keva was raving about earlier—and we wait as she and Josh wander around the room, filling glasses before we get started on the crab cake course.

"Seafood was a gutsy move," he says. "Aren't you worried about the shop smelling like a fish market tomorrow?"

"Keva assures me it's only *bad* seafood that smells, and that fresh seafood like she's selected has no smell at all as long as we take out the trash immediately after."

"You believe her?"

"Not particularly." I pick up a cracker, which is the only edible thing on the table. "But I comfort myself knowing that if we go out of business because it smells like fish, the building owner will be the one who has to deal with it. Oh wait—you'll just tear it down."

His expression has been light and easy all night, but he tenses at that, and I actually regret it. On one hand, I want to remember that he's the enemy, why he's here in the first place.

On the other hand . . . I'm sort of enjoying myself. Too much.

"How about a work truce?" he says. "Just for tonight, no discussion of business."

"Done," I say gratefully.

"So," he says with a boyish grin. "*My* turn for the invasive personal questions. How are things with your guy? Or girl?"

"Guy. And they're . . ." I smile a little wistfully as I try to explain the strange combination of feelings I get when I think of Sir. The butterflies. The old-fashioned romance of it all. The giddiness when I have a new message.

The frustration that he's not real.

"Ah," Sebastian says. His voice is just slightly curt, and I look up in question.

"It's like that," he says.

"Like what?"

"The dopey-in-love thing."

"*Dopey*?" I repeat, outraged.

"Not dopey," he amends quickly. "It's just clear he's important to you."

"Yes. He is."

"You said last time that it was complicated. What's complicated about it? He doesn't feel the same?"

I give him an annoyed look. "*Love* that that's your first assumption. But actually . . . I don't really know how he feels."

"You could ask him," he says, holding out his glass for Robyn to fill. I do the same, ignoring the blatantly curious look she gives us before moving away.

"Oh really? I could ask him?" I say sarcastically, with no heat.

"I'm just saying, men aren't exactly known for their emotive skills in this area."

"True. I should. It's just . . . ." I wrinkle my nose in befuddlement. "Why am I talking about this with you? I haven't talked about him this much with anyone."

"It's just what?" he presses, turning and pushing the plate out of the way, leaning against the counter so he's facing me.

"What if I'm disappointed?" I say it quickly, to get the words out for the first time ever. To him, of all people. Not to Rachel, or Keva, or Lily, or May, but to Sebastian Andrews.

"What do you mean?"

I blow out a breath, gathering my thoughts. "It's hard to explain. But I've built this guy up so much in my head, and I think maybe the reason I haven't pushed to move forward is that I'm worried fantasy won't match reality." I wince. "You think I'm an idiot."

"I don't," he says quietly, looking down at his glass. "I think I understand it more than you think."

"Okay, so here's another fear," I say, the bubbly apparently starting to go to my head. "And brace yourself, because this is high school–crush territory, but . . . what if he doesn't like me as much as I like him?"

Sebastian nods slowly. "I get that too. It's not high school territory. It's *human* territory. Nobody wants to learn they're the only one feeling things."

Our eyes lock for a moment that feels . . . important, somehow.

We both look away.

"So, how did you and Mr. Complicated meet?" he asks as he accepts the basket of ingredients for the crab cake from Josh. "Blind date? Mutual friend? Dating app?"

Oh, you know, we haven't actually met.

I may be sharing things with this man that I haven't with anyone else, but I draw the line at *that* humiliating little tidbit.

"You know," I say slowly as we begin unloading panko, eggs, and crab meat from the basket, "until just a couple weeks ago, I was so sure there was only one right person for everyone and that my guy would find me, Princess Jasmine–style. Or I'd find him, Little Mermaid–style."

He lifts his eyebrows. "You think you're going to rescue your soul mate from a shipwreck?"

I grin. "Mr. Andrews! Your knowledge of Disney impresses me."

"I try." He inspects a lemon, and I hope he doesn't plan to slaughter it like he did the last one. Aqua eyes cut back to mine. "And you've found him? Or he you?"

"Well, that's the thing—it feels like it, but I don't want to be wrong." I pick up a red bell pepper and sniff it distractedly, then turn to him. "You ever feel completely convinced you're supposed to be with someone but have no idea how to go about it?"

"Actually. Yes. Twice," he admits. "You?"

"Yeah." My voice is quiet now, nearly a whisper. "Twice."

His eyes darken in what seems to be irritation or . . . *jealousy?*

Keva starts explaining the art of the crab cake, and I

quickly turn away from Sebastian and walk to the front table to watch the demonstration.

Partially because I need all the cooking help I can get.

Partially because I can't let Sebastian Andrews know that for a split second on a Manhattan sidewalk, I'd thought *he* was that guy.

Sebastian and I stare at our sad excuse for a strawberry parfait.

"I thought she said it would be easy," Sebastian says, sounding vaguely accusatory.

"I thought she said we couldn't possibly do worse than the crab cake," I add.

He hands me a spoon. "Together this time?"

I take it reluctantly. "Do we have to?"

"It's just berries in some orange gunk and cream whipped with almond flavor. How bad can it be?"

I sigh and take the spoon.

"One," he counts as our spoons tip into the parfait glass in unison. "Two . . ."

We lift the spoons to our mouths.

"Three—"

So bad. So so so so bad, that's how bad it can be.

He hands me my water glass, then reaches for his own. "Jesus."

"Yeah, in case it wasn't clear, you guys get an F," Keva calls over her shoulder as she heads toward the front door, arms full of cooking equipment.

Sebastian looks affronted. "I've never failed anything in my life."

"I have," I say cheerfully, a little loose from the champagne, though I was careful not to have too much. Lowering defenses around this man feels . . . dangerous.

"What'd you fail?" he asks curiously.

"Psych. Freshman year of college. It's not worth the long story, but short version: you'll get over it."

Since Sebastian and my cooking efforts were among the worst of the group, most everyone else had cleared out before us. Grady arrived with his catering truck, and all but two of the wheeled kitchen island stations had already been moved out of the space. Still, there's plenty of cleanup to be done to get the store back to rights before opening tomorrow, and I begin to gather the champagne flutes on our station. Since we've rented them for the night, they just need to be rinsed and put back into the crate.

Robyn comes out of nowhere and takes them both out of my hand. "I've got this."

I blink at her. Never, in the nearly two years she has been working here, has she initiated helping with the more menial tasks around the store.

"That lipstick *really* suits you," I say, referring to more than the way the color lights up her face.

"Thanks!" she says brightly. "Keva says it's a tad too warm for my complexion, so we're going shopping on Saturday for something with more blue undertones. And how did you not tell me she knows the somm from Blago over on Third? He's gorgeous, single, and Keva's going to try to set us up."

I can only blink at her, wondering where the Robyn I've known—and let's be honest, suffered through—for almost five years has gone.

I'm also increasingly aware that Sebastian is still here, the only nonemployee in the space. And that it doesn't feel weird. Maybe because I know he's the landlord of sorts? Though shouldn't that make it *more* weird?

I feel Robyn's gaze flick between me and Sebastian, her speculation clear, and when I try to pick up our failed strawberry parfait, she blocks me. "Why don't you head out for the night, boss. You've been setting up all day for the class."

"We all have," I argue.

"Yes, but you also did the planning and the organizing and lost enough sleep for all of us."

"I didn't lose sleep!" I did. I definitely lost sleep, because everything we do in the store seems to matter too much. One slip, one bad sales day, one slow week . . .

But the most alarming part is that there are moments when I wonder if the store failing wouldn't be a blessing in disguise.

Hands full of dirty dishes, Robyn heads toward the front of the store, and I glance at Sebastian. He's already removed his apron, making me realize I'm still wearing mine. I tug the string around my waist and lift my arms to pull the thing over my head, then yelp as I inadvertently tug the baby hairs at the back of my neck.

Wordlessly, Sebastian moves behind me. "You're tangled," he mutters softly. "Hold on."

He pushes my hair over my shoulder to better see what

he's doing. I don't move a muscle as his warm fingers brush the sensitive skin on the back of my neck. I feel the ever-so-slight scrape of a short nail as he works, feel the heat of his body in the too-warm room.

"There we go," he murmurs, lifting the apron over my head. No tug this time.

"Thank you," I say, not quite looking at him. "Apparently I don't know how to work aprons, but good thing you're handy with them."

"A waste of a skill considering the result," he says, pointing at the melting parfait that looks like a foamy chem lab experiment gone wrong.

"I hope everyone else had better luck," I say a little glumly. "I'd hate to think we charged people three hundred bucks for food they can't even eat."

"Pretty sure we were the only ones who were three for three on inedibility. Everyone else seemed to be having a great time, and at least got fed."

"You really think so?" I look up at him. I tell myself his approval matters for professional reasons, but the way my heart thumps says otherwise.

He shrugs. "Sure. Yeah. Nobody seemed to be leaving hungry."

"Nobody but you."

He smiles slightly. "I confess, I'm a bit peckish."

"Is that a nice way of saying you're starving? Because I *so* am." I tilt the basket of crackers toward me, but it's long empty, the only thing I've eaten since the burrito I had for lunch while setting up.

Sebastian had rolled up his dress sleeves while we worked—and no, the distraction of his toned forearms had nothing to do with my cooking mishaps, why do you ask?—but he's rolled them back down now and is rebuttoning the cuffs in a gesture so effortlessly masculine my mouth goes a bit dry.

"So feed me," he says simply, reaching out and picking up the suit jacket he's folded over the back of a chair, out of range of our cooking disaster.

"Sorry?" I ask, still distracted, as he shrugs on the navy jacket. At some point during the evening he'd loosened his tie, just a little, and unbuttoned the top button. I wait for him to button it, to tighten the knot, but he does neither. This is a more relaxed Mr. Andrews.

This is *Sebastian*, I realize.

"Feed me," he says with a slight smile. "I want my money's worth."

"You had *excellent* champagne. Hardly a rip-off."

"True. But I did sign up for a cooking class. I believe the website indicated a three-course meal was included." He reaches for his phone. "I could check . . ."

"Oh my God, fine. I'll refund you 50 percent. Which is more than fair, since you did drink the wine, and that was the most expensive part."

The light in his eyes dims. "Forget it. I wasn't asking for a refund."

"Then what—"

Now he does button his shirt. Tightens the knot of his tie. "Thanks for the interesting evening, Ms. Cooper."

I feel my heart sink. That brief glimpse of Sebastian the

man is gone, and just like that, he's back to being the buttoned-up Mr. Andrews.

He strides away without looking back, pausing at the front door and stepping aside to make way for Keva and Grady's re-entry, then exits into the night.

I feel something thwack against my chest, glance down, and see my purse and May's magenta nails. "Gracie. We'll clean up. Go feed that boy."

There are plenty of things I could and should say. That the cooking class was my idea, and I'd clean up. That *they* should go home and I'll take care of the rest.

That Sebastian was hardly a boy.

That he wasn't mine to feed.

That he wasn't mine *period*.

Instead, I give her a quick hug of gratitude, then find my-self out on Central Park South, looking both right and left as I realize it's unlikely he'd return to the office at this hour, and I have no idea if he lives on the East or West Side.

Luckily, the street's relatively quiet at this hour on a week-night, and I catch sight of his broad shoulders moving toward Broadway. He's got a long stride, so I have to speed walk, and even then, I can't quite catch up to him unless I run. And my clunky sandals aren't going to cooperate with that.

"Mr. Andrews!"

He doesn't turn. Or even pause.

"Sebastian!"

He halts and slowly pivots toward me, waiting as I close the distance between us. He looks down at me, those aqua eyes questioning, maybe a little wary.

I smile. "I can't afford fancy. But how do you feel about Halal?" I tilt my head toward the circle of food stands in Columbus Circle.

Something warm and wonderful happens to his face that takes my breath away.

I keep babbling to disguise my reaction. "It's a little over-priced since it's in tourist central, but their gyros are pretty great for absorbing excess champagne."

"Speaking from experience?" he asks as we walk toward the food stand in silent agreement.

"I was born and bred into the sparkling wine business, so yeah, I know my way around hangover prevention."

He glances down at me. "Did you ever want to do any-thing else besides go into the family business?"

I smile. "Of course. Didn't you?"

"Of course."

I look up at his profile, then away. "Astronaut? Doctor? Fireman?"

"A jockey."

I laugh and give his six-foot-plus frame a once-over. "Seri-ously?"

"When I was eleven and a business partner had given my parents tickets to a fancy box at the Kentucky Derby. I'd barely even seen a horse before then, but I was fascinated and decided there'd be no cooler job than flying around a muddy track on horseback."

"How long did the dream last?" I ask as we step behind a couple of teens in line at the Halal food truck.

"Longer than you'd guess. My mom had gently pointed

out that jockeys were usually of a certain height and that genetics might not be in my favor, but I did my research. The average jockey was about five two, of which I was perfectly in range at the time. But then . . ."

"Growth spurt?" I ask.

He nods. "A big one. I went from five feet to six feet overnight."

"Crushing."

"A little bit. Though making the varsity baseball team as a sophomore helped ease the disappointment."

"And I'm sure it didn't hurt that the prep school girls, after years of towering above the boys, were delighted by your growth spurt?"

He smiles a little and doesn't deny it. "It did not hurt."

Sebastian and I step up to order. He studies the menu, then glances down at me. "I'll have what you're having."

"Spicy sauce or no?"

"Yes, but don't go crazy."

"Not one of those people who needs to order extra heat to prove your badassery?"

"Do those people exist?"

"Oh yes. Most of my ex-boyfriends," I say, smiling at the man behind the counter. "Hey, Omer."

"Gracie! Where you been? Everything good?"

"Everything's great! Just busy, but in the good way. How are things here?"

"Same great days, great nights. No complaints. Same thing?"

"Yep, but make it two. And two waters."

Sebastian reaches to pull out his wallet, but I place my hand on his, trying to ignore the way the simple contact makes my pulse leap. "You told me to feed you. Let me do it."

I brace for him to argue. I want to do this, to show him I'm not some floundering shop owner, but a businesswoman who's built something. It's important to me.

Slowly, he nods.

Omer gives me my change, and I stuff all of it into the plastic tip cup. Grabbing two bottles of water out of the ice at the front of the stand, I step aside to let the couple behind us place their order while our food cooks, and Sebastian follows my lead.

He twists off the cap of his water and takes a drink, then replaces it. "What did you want to be?"

I'd been distracted by a saxophonist playing a decent version of "It Had to be You" and turn back toward him. "What?"

"Before you decided to be a champagne shop owner. What did you want to be?"

"Oh. An artist."

Sebastian says nothing, his attention seemingly on the saxophonist as well. He surprises me by handing me his water, then pulling a twenty out of his wallet and dropping it into the man's case, a lone twenty among a pile of ones and a couple of fives. The man pauses in his playing to flash a gap-toothed smile at Sebastian. "Thank you."

Sebastian nods, then turns back to me with a mischievous grin. "Well, well. Another twenty-dollar bill."

"Any more, and I won't be able to see one without thinking of you," I say before I can think better of it.

Something flits across Sebastian's face at my words, but Omer waves me over to get the food before I can identify it.

Central Park is open until midnight, but the nights are slowly growing chillier, so there are fewer people here after dark than in the peak of summer. We find a bench and sit. I'm too hungry to make decent small talk, and the first bite has my eyes rolling back in my head.

"Good, right?" I say, mouth full as I look at Sebastian, who's already devoured three bites.

He nods slowly and wipes his mouth with a thin paper napkin. He brings the gyro to his mouth as though to take another bite, then frowns at it. "So why didn't you?"

"Why didn't I what?"

"Become an artist." He takes another bite.

I shrug. "Probably the same reason most midwestern eighteen-year-olds who move to Hollywood don't ever get to go to the Oscars. Some things are simply meant to be dreams."

"What kind of artist are you?"

"I dabble," I say vaguely, not in the mood to revisit the cutesy Tinker Bell comment when things are so amiable between us.

"Did you ever try? To go professional?"

"Did *you* ever try?"

"To become a horse jockey?"

I smile. "No. To be anything other than—what's your title again? Vice president of city domination?"

He winces. "Development. Vice president of development."

"Same thing," I mutter, wiping some hot sauce from the back of my hand. Out of the corner of my eye, I see a frustrated look cross his face, and he exhales before taking another bite.

We chew in silence for several moments. Not quite tense, not quite comfortable. As though we both know we're constantly straddling a line between tentative truce and opposing goals.

When he speaks again, he's apparently chosen to lean into the truce, because he looks and sounds more relaxed than usual. "I haven't done this in a long time."

"The food? The park? The bench?" I ask curiously.

"All of it. The spontaneity, mostly."

"You do seem to be rather . . . structured."

"Wouldn't you be?" he says, mostly to himself. "If you'd grown up hearing, even jokingly, that you were betrothed from the cradle? If there was a Princeton sweatshirt under the tree every Christmas, long before you'd even thought about college? If it was a foregone conclusion that you'd take over the family business?"

"So where *did* you go to college?"

"Princeton."

I think about this as I finish my gyro. I crumple up the foil as I chew the last bite, knowing I did Omer proud with my eating, even if I disgraced Keva with my cooking.

"I know I only met them once," I say cautiously. "But your

parents seem pretty cool. Reasonable. You can't undo the Princeton thing, but you could marry this other girl—the complicated one. Become a horse trainer because, sorry, you've got to give up the jockey thing. You're way too big."

He crumples up his own foil and then twists it idly in his fingers, lost in thought. "Perhaps."

"You want to know what I think?" I turn toward him and pull my leg up beneath me, prop my elbow up on the back of the bench so I can look at this complicated man.

"Oddly, yes."

I don't mind the *oddly* part. I know what he means. We're not friends. On a professional front, we're downright adversaries. But we're connected somehow, and that sense that I knew him even before I met him seems to grow stronger the more I'm with him. Might as well put my inexplicable connection to this man to good use.

"I think it's easier to go along with what your parents want. Easy, in a comfortable sort of way. If you're chasing what they want, and it doesn't quite work out, the loss would be tempered somewhat. You won't fight for it as hard, true, but it also won't sting as much because you've got no skin in the game."

He crumples the ball in his left fist, then leans back on the bench, his right elbow brushing mine lightly as he stretches out his legs. "No, I don't believe that's true."

"You don't?" I'm surprised. I'd sort of impressed myself with my insight.

He shakes his head and looks over at me. "No. If we were

less motivated by other people's plans for us, by other people's dreams, you wouldn't be fighting so hard to keep Bubbles & More open."

My head snaps back, a little stung that he'd upset our truce by going there. "It's not the same."

"No?" He pivots toward me, leaning his head against his fist, mirroring my posture. "So, if Bubbles *hadn't* been a family run store, you'd still refuse to even hear my offer? Still refuse to consider something that might be better for your employees. And for you?"

"Respectfully, you don't know the first thing about what's right for me, Mr. Andrews."

He frowns a little, more to himself than at me, and lifts his head slightly. His finger beside mine on the bench moves closer. Just slightly enough that it could be an accident. But then the tip of his small finger brushes mine, a whisper of a touch.

"No," he says quietly. "Perhaps not."

Yearning.

It's the first word that pops into my head, and it's also one that makes me think of Sir. And the realization that I'm thinking of one man while sitting beside another, that for the first time in my life I feel it for two men, and can have neither, leaves me frustrated.

I stand abruptly. "It's late. I should be heading home."

Sebastian doesn't argue. "Sure," he replies, standing up as well.

We walk in silence toward the park exit. "Where do you live? I'll walk you home."

I smile. "I appreciate that, but I've walked myself home hundreds of times."

His stubborn expression doesn't change, and I roll my eyes but smile. "Hell's Kitchen. Fifty-Fourth, between Ninth and Tenth. I doubt you're going my way."

"I'm not. But I'll walk you home. But first . . ." He points at one of the food stands. "Ice cream."

"You know, I think you made all that up about your parental pressures," I joke. "I don't think there's ever been anything you wanted that you didn't get."

"You'd be surprised," he says quietly, then points at the menu. "What are you having? My treat."

Not saying no to that. I survey the menu. No pistachio gelato, but I could easily make do with something chocolatey. Or maybe just a basic vanilla *dipped* in chocolate and sprinkled with some peanuts. Or . . .

My gaze locks on a menu item in the bottom right corner. It's a whole subcategory of frozen treats I've never bothered with before because there's no chocolate, no nuts, no flavor . . .

You haven't lived until you've tried a lemon sorbet on a hot summer day in the city . . .

It's not a hot summer day in the city, but . . .

I point. "I'll have one of those."

The look he gives me is so long, and so piercing, I think I've offended his very soul. A sentiment I can agree with, because I've sort of just offended myself as well. Lemon sorbet? Really?

Sebastian turns toward the impatient woman waiting to take our order. "Two lemon sorbet cups, please."

The order bothers me. Lemon sorbet is my thing with Sir, and I don't like thinking about Sebastian Andrews and Sir in the same thought.

I like even less that when he notices me shiver and drops his coat over my shoulders, I stop thinking about Sir altogether.

Fourteen

It's been a while since I've indulged in a proper girls' night. And when you need one? You *need* one.

I've invited all the usual suspects: Lily, Rachel, and Keva, but I've also made a surprising addition:

Robyn.

The prickly sommelier's been bothering me less lately. The intensity that used to drive me, well, *nuts*, has actually been a pretty big asset around the store lately. I'm realizing that perhaps I've been seeing her all wrong: Robyn's not a condescending know-it-all as much as she is a woman who's lucky enough to have found her passion (sparkling wine) and a job that allows her to live that passion.

In the past couple of weeks, it's been Robyn who stays late to help me brainstorm new ideas on increasing revenue; Robyn who takes it upon herself to try to get vendor sponsorships every Friday; Robyn who's taken over inventory management.

And I don't know if it's the successful shopping trip with Keva that resulted in her new lipstick or what, but her customer service skills have done an about-face. Instead of spouting off her knowledge as though wanting a gold star for her efforts, she comes across as committed to making sure people take home a wine they love.

She's even been friendlier with the Bubbles team and had nearly broken my heart last week when she'd shyly confessed that she'd never been good at making friends and had asked for tips. Remembering the look of pleased shock on her face when I'd invited her to tonight's get-together is making it a *little* easier to tolerate the fact that she's currently in my living room rattling on about the flavor profile of vodka.

Lily catches my eye from the kitchen, where she's adding baby carrots and ranch dip to her plate, and makes a face as Robyn utters the word *grain alcohol* for the tenth time, but she's smiling.

"Oh *gawd*," Keva interrupts Robyn, reaching out and emptying the remains of the cocktail shaker into Robyn's glass. "Woman, I love talking about my craft too, but at some point, food is just food, and a drink is just a drink." She points. "So drink it and shut up."

Robyn, cross-legged on my living room floor, blinks. Then she shrugs and sips her cocktail. "Okay."

"I'm so glad I pumped my afternoon away so I could drink," Rachel says, pulling her curly hair into a messy knot atop her head. "I had no idea how great cosmos were. I thought they were just a *Sex and the City* set piece."

"Take it from someone who came of age during their heyday, there's such a thing as too many," Lily says, returning to the living room with a glass of white wine.

The other women all happily sip the cosmopolitans I suggested. Paintings with pink cocktails are continually my best sellers, and every now and then I get a craving.

Lily dunks a potato chip in the ranch meant for her untouched carrots, and after popping it into her mouth, wipes the salt off her fingers and makes grabby hands in Rachel's direction. "Okay. Show me *all* the baby pictures."

"Oh gosh," Rachel says, picking up the phone sitting near her hip on the couch. "I don't know if I have . . . *less than five million*."

I'm on Rachel's family album, so I've seen all the highlights already, but Robyn and Keva crowd around Lily as she flips through the photos, the three of them gushing about dimples and chunky baby thighs. Rachel looks over at me and rolls her eyes, but she's smiling.

Lily's smile is bright and genuine, but there's a wistfulness in her eyes. It must be bittersweet—Rachel has three, Lily doesn't even have one.

Robyn heaves out a sigh. "Ugh. I want one."

"Me too," Keva says. "In, like, thirty years. When either science will have evolved so that old ladies can have them when they're good and ready, or, ooh, maybe robots can carry our children."

I wince. Keva doesn't know about Lily's fertility struggles, and thus doesn't mean to be insensitive, but my heart aches for my sister anyway. I reach a foot out under the coffee table and rub my fuzzy sock against Lily's. My sister smiles at me and wiggles her toes back in reassurance. *It's okay.* A leftover gesture from childhood movie nights when one of us sensed the other was sad about Mom.

"Keva, if you find a childbearing robot, hook me up," Lily says.

Keva salutes in acknowledgment, and Robyn turns toward me.

"What about you, Gracie?" she asks. "Babies in your future?"

"Are you kidding?" Lily interjects. "She'd *better*. I happen to know for a fact that Gracie's had her ideal family planned out since before she got boobs."

I laugh and steal one of my sister's carrots. "It's totally true. A boy, Griffin, my mom's maiden name. And a little girl, Ella."

"After . . ."

"Cinderella," Rachel answers for me. "Be grateful I talked her out of *Snow*, as in White."

"Fairy-tale buff?" Robyn asks curiously.

"Just a romantic," I say, ignoring the twin snorts from Rachel and Lily, who've known me long enough to know it's an understatement.

"So what about Griffin and Ella's dad?" Robyn asks curiously. "Wait, no, I know this one. Tall, dark, and handsome, may or may not own a white horse? Ooh, or blond, like Thor?"

Keva, Rachel, and Lily answer for me at the same time. "Medium-height musician, long hair, warm brown eyes, crooked smile, and a dad bod."

I take a sip of my cosmopolitan and play along goodnaturedly. "I refuse to be shamed for having specific standards. He's out there."

"Wait," Robyn says. "He doesn't even exist?"

I think of Sir. "He does."

I'm pretty sure.

"Hmm" Keva says thoughtfully. "But are you sure about Mr. Right's eye color?"

I glare at her in warning.

She grins back, unrepentant. "I'm just saying, are you sure they're brown? Or are they a rather unique shade of Tiffany blue?"

"Oooh what am I missing?" Rachel says, leaning forward eagerly.

Robyn fans herself. "Sebastian Andrews. This hot businessman who's got a thing for Gracie. He's shown up to two events, and both times, he couldn't keep those sexy blue eyes off her."

Lily and I exchange a look—I haven't told anyone besides my siblings and May that Sebastian's primary interest in Bubbles & More is to see it shut down.

As to his secondary interest . . .

I don't let my mind go that way. I've been trying really hard not to think of the way Sebastian's coat had felt around my shoulders. The way the warmth and smell had made me feel safe.

Or the fact that he may have broken things off with Genevieve, but there's still some other mystery woman in the picture.

Whom I hate.

"What about your MysteryMate guy?" Rachel asks.

"Wait, what?" Robyn and my sister say at the same time.

I give Rachel an exasperated look, and she gives me a sheepish grin. "Sorry. Too many cosmos, not enough lunch."

When my sister kicks my foot under the table, it's less gentle this time. "What's she talking about?"

"Just this guy I met on a dating app," I say as casually as I can.

"*Haven't* met," Keva clarifies. "But that she's halfway in love with."

"Wait," Lily holds up a hand. "Are you telling me that my baby sister's top romantic prospects are a guy who's bullying her to close the family business and someone she hasn't even *met*?"

I sigh, and giving into the inevitable, bring everybody up to speed on both the Sebastian/Bubbles situation and the Sir situation.

"Good God, Gracie," Robyn sounds horrified. "First, that Sebastian has been lurking around like some vulture waiting to pounce as soon as you fail. And that you're being *catfished*."

"Seriously," Lily chimes in. "He could be a nineteen-year-old who lives with his mother. Or a forty-eight-year-old."

"Or not a *him* at all," Rachel says. "What if this is a teenage mean girl messing with you?"

"Is nobody on my side here?" I ask.

"I am," Keva says immediately. "I've never seen you as happy as when you found this pen pal guy." She pauses. "Though, now that I think about it, you did have a distinct glow at that cooking thing with Sebastian."

"So who are we rooting for?" Robyn asks, looking around the room.

"Neither," I say. "Sebastian and I are just . . ." *Rivals? Friends? Might have been but will never be?*

"He's seeing someone," I say, since I honestly don't know

how to explain the complexity of my feelings for the man, or my increasing resentment that he's pretty flirty for someone who's hung up on another woman.

On the other hand, am I one to talk? I have feelings for two men, neither of whom are even available.

Except Sir might be.

This, I realize, is what girls' nights are meant for.

I wait until Keva's refilled everyone's drink before bringing the group up to speed on Sir's single status.

"Well, obviously, you have to meet him," Keva says.

"You do," Lily says, surprising me.

"Seriously?" Rachel says to my sister. "That is not what I thought you were going to say."

Lily shrugs. "I mean, Gracie, if he tells you to go out to his place in Long Island City at 11 p.m. and to bring large garbage bags with you, then yeah, *abort mission*. But if you're smart about it and meet him in a bright, public place with plenty of people around, and don't start the conversation by rattling off your social security number . . ." She shrugs.

"That's true," Robyn chimes in. "It's really no different than any other dating app in that way."

"Except she doesn't know what he looks like," the everskeptical Rachel points out.

"Which is not unlike a blind date," Keva says.

"I dunno," Rachel says, picking up one of Keva's mushroom crostini and nibbling it thoughtfully. "I'm still kind of rooting for the other guy. He sounds hot."

"But maybe Sir is hot too. She'll never know unless she meets him," Keva argues.

"Okay, I'm shutting this down," I say, making an X motion with my arms. "Neither of them is my guy. Sebastian is unavailable, and even if he weren't, he'll lose interest in Bubbles the second he learns we're not going to move out and let him build his skyscraper. And Sir's never made the slightest indication that he wants to take our relationship to the next level."

"Have you ever given him any indication that *you* might?" Lily asks gently. "I've seen how you are around guys, Gracie. You become everybody's insta best friend, but you don't realize you give off the vibe that you *only* want to be friends."

"That's not true!" I protest. "Nobody wants a relationship as much as me, you guys know that."

"Maybe that's the problem," Robyn suggests. "You've built it up so much in your head that you're afraid the reality won't measure up, so you keep everyone at arm's length. It's also probably why you're so attracted to a guy you've never met. It lets you preserve that dream."

"That's . . ."

Of all the women in the room, I know Robyn the least. Which is why it's all the more jarring that she's just managed to sum up my entire romantic life in one simple, spot-on assessment.

I've been priding myself so long on my high standards . . .

But what if the reality is much less commendable?

What if I'm simply scared to death of being disappointed?

My dear Lady,

I realize our relationship, if I might call it that, is one that's free of expectation, so I hope this won't come across as overstepping, but are you okay? I haven't heard from you in a while and wanted to let you know I'm here.

Yours in concern,

Sir

Fifteen

The higher you fly, the harder you fall.

I never quite understood that phrase, but when you live it? You know.

I've run the numbers. I've done the math. I've repeated the process over and over, praying for a different result, and each time, the reality feels colder and more final.

Surely I'm doing something wrong. Missing something.

I call my brother-in-law.

It says everything about Alec's character that even though things are tense between him and Lily, even though it's 2 p.m. in the middle of the workday, he agrees to meet me at Starbucks to double-check my accounting.

I try hard not to look at his face while he studies my laptop and instead focus on enjoying my pumpkin spice Frappuccino. I have to budget my expenses pretty carefully, and Starbucks generally doesn't fit into my day-to-day, or even weekly, expenditures. I reserve fancy beverages like this one for birthday splurges or celebrations. Today is neither, but when Alec offered to pay, I hadn't been able to resist.

I need something good to come from this day, and if it's limited to a sweet treat that tastes like fall, I'll take it.

Alec is the quiet, serious type. He takes his time. Sips his tea. Adjusts his glasses.

Finally, he looks up.

And I know.

I know.

I've always known.

I push the drink forward, staring at the streak of condensation left on the wooden table. "Bubbles isn't going to make it."

"It could. You're still technically profitable." He says it calmly, quietly, and I'm grateful. I don't want a pep talk any more than I want a lecture. "But the sort of improvement you, Lily, and Caleb were hoping for isn't there."

I close my eyes and exhale.

"You should be proud, Gracie," he says, shutting the laptop. "When you took over after Howie died, I didn't think the store had a shot in hell of staying open. Your dad was smart and passionate, but he didn't pivot as soon as he should have to adjust for changing times. You turned it around."

"I *turned* it," I clarify. "Not around. Not enough."

I set three fingertips against the center of my forehead and close my eyes. "What do I do, Alec?" I ask quietly, looking up into his brown eyes. As a teen, my brother-in-law had been quiet and even a little aloof, though incredibly kind once you got to know him. He grew out of the aloofness, but not the kindness. He's the type of man you can count on.

He picks up his cup of tea and stares down at it a minute

before sighing and reaching for my sugary pumpkin-flavored drink. He takes a sip then studies the drink. "I can't decide if I like this or not."

"It grows on you. A little too much," I say as he slides it back toward me and lifts his own cup once more.

"You do what you want to do, Gracie."

I make a little face at the vagueness of the answer.

He gives a slight shake of his head. "I'm not talking about what you want for the business. I'm talking what you want for your life."

The question churns something deep inside me. To deflect, I reach across the table and give his forearm a sisterly poke. "Hey, look at you! Speaking from personal experience, or just been brushing up on your Oprah vibes?"

He smiles, but his eyes are shadowed as he looks down at his drink. "Let's just say you're not the only whose life didn't play out quite like you planned it."

Instantly, I feel like the worst sister on the planet, and this time my hand on his arm is less playful, more comforting. "I should have asked sooner. How are you?"

His brown gaze is so tormented when it lifts it hurts my heart. "You've talked to your sister?"

I raise a shoulder in confirmation. There's a tricky line between help and interference, and I don't want to betray Lily's confidence.

Alec drags a hand over his face. "How am I? Hmm. I'm frustrated. I don't know where her head's at. I don't know what she wants. I don't know if I'm supposed to bring home adoption papers or the name of a different doctor . . ."

"What do you want?" I ask, repeating his question back to him.

He exhales. "I want to have a family. I want my wife to know she is my family, even if it's only ever meant to be the two of us. I want to give her a million babies, if that's what she wants, however I can . . ."

Alec looks at me helplessly.

I place my palms on either side of my cold, damp plastic cup and roll it between my palms, watching the green straw move back and forth as I imagine dancing toward the line of interference without actually crossing it.

"Have you told her any of this? Does she know how you feel?"

He blinks at me. "She knows I love her."

Oh, men. So sweet. So clueless.

"I'm sure she does," I say with a reassuring smile. "But does she know that she's enough for you? You know how Lily is. She's never failed at anything in her life. I wonder if she's not feeling a little lost knowing that she might not be meant to bear children naturally. I wonder if she doesn't just need to know that you're there."

He's quiet for a moment. "I should cut back on the travel is what you're saying."

I smile, and Alec nods. *Point taken.* He gestures toward my drink. "Can I have some more of that?"

I shove it toward him, and he takes a long sip, winces, studies the cup. Then takes another sip. "Yes. Yes, I do like this. Now, back to you. Do you want to run Bubbles for the rest of your life? Because if that's what you want, I'll help however I can. The numbers don't tell a great story, but it's possible this is just a bad chapter."

I look down at my thumbnails, at the chipped pink polish I probably should have removed three days ago.

"I know what I *don't* want," I say, still not looking up.

"That's a start. Let's hear it."

"I don't want to break my promise to Dad. I don't want to disappoint Lily and Caleb."

"And that's enough for you?"

He asks it gently, curiously, but I can't bring myself to answer, not out loud. I don't want to answer.

But somewhere deep inside me, the answer whispers anyway. *No. That's not good enough.* I want to be brave enough to go after what my heart wants.

I want to be bold. Daring.

Happy.

I take a deep breath, both exhilarated and terrified when I realize what I have to do.

To Sir, out on a shaky limb,

I apologize for the radio silence. I've been sorting through some of the messier bits of being human as of late. Do you ever ask yourself the big questions and realize you don't have a clear answer? What sort of person do I want to be? What sort of life do I want to have? *With* whom do I want to live that life?

I know I'm a kind person, or at least I try to be, but I'm also realizing I'm bit of a chicken in a lot of ways. More obsessed with the dream than doing the work to make the dream a reality.

I live a good life—I do. But I'm learning it's a life lived largely for the people around me, to support their expectations, to never rock the boat, to never let anyone down. I feel trapped, but how does one find that balance—to be true to oneself without being selfish?

The one area I've always thought I was in control of, the one area lived for me, by my standards, is my personal, romantic life. And I know I'm overstepping our usual topics of conversation, but I feel I've misstepped here as well. I'm alone, and on some level, I've always known that's of my own making, but now I can't help but wonder if there are opportunities missed, chances lost, connections I never let happen.

I'm rambling now. This is the longest message I've ever sent, by far, and I apologize if I'm destroying what we have, moving us from pithy quips to something altogether a bit more maudlin. Especially since I haven't shared this with anyone in my "real" life, which I guess leads me to this:

Life feels most real when I'm writing to you, when I see your screen name in my in-box. I don't know your name. Your face. Your age. But I have the sense I know *you*. And that you know me too, in a way perhaps nobody else does.

So if nothing else, even if I've scared you away, I want you to know that when I'm old and withered, saggy and gray, I will look back on these days, and you, my friend, will be a bright spot.

Lady

———————

My dear Lady,

I'm not quite sure where to begin. I suppose, most obviously, you haven't scared me away. You haven't ruined things. I'm here. And perhaps now it's me who's making things weird, but I have a hard time imagining a version of my life where I won't be here for you, however you need me.

You're real to me too. You're important to me.

I'm honored to be your confidant. Everything you're saying is valuable, and I mean this when I say: relatable.

I mentioned recently that I ended a relationship. The truth is that relationship had run its course long ago, but I'd stayed in it for the sake of someone else. In that way, I suppose leaving the relationship *was* selfish, and I know I left disappointment in the wake of that breakup. But I also know that we get only so many trips around the sun. Having "met" you, I know that on as many of those days as possible, I want to feel the way I feel when I see your screen name in my in-box.

Yours in have I ruined this?

Sir

_____

To Sir, with an aching throat,

You've ruined nothing. Indeed, you've only made whatever we have a bit more lovely. And it's here that I take the biggest risk of all:

Would you like to meet?

Lady

Sixteen

He doesn't write back. Not that day. Not the next.

Three days later, I still haven't heard from Sir.

I try to tell myself it doesn't matter. It shouldn't matter. I tell myself over and over that a person I don't even know shouldn't have that much power over my happiness.

But I meant what I said in my last message. I *do* know him. It's silly, it's romantic, it's maybe straight-up nuts, but I know in the depths of my heart that I've shared parts of myself with him that I've never shared with anyone. And I thought it had been the same for him.

I thought there was something special, but maybe . . .

Maybe what made it feel so special was the illusion of it all. To Robyn's point at girls' night, maybe I really am just clinging to the fantasy of him so I won't have to deal with the fact that life is disappointing more often than not.

But none of this makes his rejection easier to take.

A little after eight, a week after my Starbucks meeting with Alec, he opens the front door to his and Lily's apartment to let me in. "Hey," he says, pecking my cheek. "Come on in. Lil's just putting some snacks together."

"Hey, Gracie!" she calls from the kitchen.

"Where's May?" I ask, shrugging out of my coat and handing it over to Alec.

"She had to bail," Lily replies. "Has a stomach bug that she described in way more detail than I needed, but insists we record the entire family chat and send it to her after so she doesn't miss the *deets*. Her word."

"Something to drink, G?" Alec asks, going to the fridge.

"Water—bubbly if you've got it."

"Lemon or plain?"

"Lemon."

"Lily?" Alec asks, not looking at his wife as he pulls out a can of sparkling water for me.

"I'll have some of that merlot from last night, thanks."

They don't look at each other during the exchange, and I stifle a sigh. Maybe it's a good thing I'm about to have a lot of time on my hands—helping these two fix their marriage could be a full-time job.

I help myself to a slice of baguette and some sort of garlicky mushroomy concoction that I recognize from girls' night—Lily had asked Keva for the recipe.

Alec hands Lily a glass of wine and me a tall glass with sparkling water and a lemon spiral twist draped artfully over the side. "Fancy!"

"Only the best at Chez Wyndman," he says, giving a formal butler bow before helping himself to the appetizers.

Lily's focused on wrestling open the plastic wrapping on cocktail napkins she picked up at Bubbles when she'd stopped by on Sunday after brunch with a friend. The napkins are cute.

Two girls walking arm in arm through Central Park surrounded by fall foliage. I'm glad I ordered some for the store, but the artist in me couldn't help but think about what I would have done differently had it been my design. Added a cute scarf for one of the girls, boots for the other. Maybe a leashed puppy pouncing on a leaf . . .

Alec glances at his wife a moment, then lifts his crostini and nods toward the other room. "I'll be in my office if you need me. Tell Caleb I say hey."

Lily's head snaps up, and she seems to see—*really* see—her husband for the first time since I've been here. "You're not staying for the call?"

Alec's got the crostini halfway to his mouth, but he pauses in the doorway and looks back at her. "I thought it was a family call."

Her head snaps back just slightly. "You're family." *Unless you don't want to be.*

"Not Cooper family," he replies quietly. *Unless you want me to be.*

I chew my mushrooms and refrain from rolling my eyes. If this were a cartoon, I'd smile pleasantly and bonk their heads together *just* hard enough to knock some sense into their stubborn married asses.

"Get over here," I say to Alec as I lean forward and open Lily's laptop. "You're a huge part of Bubbles *and* this family. You should be here for this discussion."

I'm sitting in the middle of the sofa, but when I see them walking toward either side of me, I quickly scoot to my left so they have to sit next to each other. Lily narrows her eyes slightly, as though trying to figure out if I'm manipulating the situation, but I feign preoccupation with getting the call set up.

Lily sits in the middle, Alec joining her on the other side just as the video chat connects and Caleb's smiling face appears.

"Oh, thank God," Caleb says when he sees Alec. "Another male presence."

"Um, I believe the *thank God* should be reserved for the fact that you got rid of that facial hair," Lily says.

He rubs his bare chin. "You think? I'm sort of missing it."

"It looked like a weed," I say, backing up my sister. "Or pubes."

"And they wonder why I moved out of state," Caleb mutters before looking back at Alec. "How are you, man? It's been a while."

"Good, good," Alec replies. "You?"

"Same. Got a new client who's sort of a pain in the ass, but the pay's good. Got a new girlfriend too."

"*What?*" Lily and I say at the same time.

"How did I not know about this?" I demand. "She better be a brand-new girlfriend, because I just talked to you two days ago, and you made no mention of this development."

He scratches his ear. "It's been a few weeks. I didn't mention it because you'd start doing that thing."

"What thing?" I scowl.

"You know. The thing where you start asking if I've met

her parents, when she's coming to New York to meet you guys, whether she wants a small intimate ceremony or if you should start looking for availabilities at St. Patrick's . . ."

Lily nods and looks my way. "You do that. Alec and I started dating when you were *nine*, and the second time he came over, you showed him a picture you'd colored. Of my wedding dress."

Alec leans forward and looks at me. "Really good drawing though." He gives me a thumbs-up.

"And my actual wedding dress did end up looking startlingly like that picture," Lily admits. "But the point is, you tend to get a little . . ."

"I'd call it aggressive fairy godmother," Caleb says.

"Okay, but was I wrong?" I say. I waggle a finger between Alec and Lily. "They did end up getting married. And," I say to Caleb, "I wasn't pushy when you were dating Missy, because I knew she wasn't the one. And Lily, just before you met Alec, that weird Dan asked you out, and did I not tell you not to bother?"

"You did."

"And did you listen?"

"Again, you were *nine*."

I lift my eyebrows, and she sighs. "No. I didn't listen."

"And what happened?"

"He took me to a party, then spent the night making out with his ex."

I lift my palms. "I rest my case."

Alec glances back at the laptop screen to Caleb. "So I'm guessing that's a no on the new girl meeting your sisters?"

"*Yeeeaaah*, I'm going to go ahead and not freak her out by having Lily ask her credit score and Gracie mailing her pictures of wedding cakes."

Lily looks at me. "Our sisterly qualities are so underappreciated."

"Totally." I look back at Caleb. "Can I at least see a picture of her? Is she pretty? Does she make you laugh? Can I call her sis? What color does she want her Christmas stocking to be?"

"Uh-oh," Caleb says, "I hope my Wi-Fi doesn't cut out on me. I just *hate* when my nightmares play all the way through to the end . . ."

"But—"

"Maybe we give poor Caleb a break and let Gracie explain why she's called the family meeting?" Alec says.

Lily and Caleb both turn their attention toward me, expectant and a little curious. I don't blame them. One of the painful self-realizations of the past few weeks is just how little of my own life I've initiated. I'm the Cooper sibling who sorts through and soothes *others'* announcements and choices. That's about to change.

I take a deep breath. "I think we should close the store."

There's a long moment of silence, followed by Lily's "Seriously?" and Caleb's "Wait, what?"

"Where is this coming from?" my sister asks. "All the effort we've put in, the new website, the cooking class—"

"You guys' help was so appreciated," I say. "And I'm glad we gave it a shot, I really am. But the store's revenue is still pretty dismal. If we don't choose to close it now, I expect we'll be forced to a year from now. And a year from now we won't have the offer from the Andrews Corporation on the table."

"We don't even know what that offer is," Caleb says. "I thought we basically told them to go to hell."

Another deep breath. "Actually, we *do* know the details of their offer. Sylvia's still on retainer, and I had her get in touch with their attorney to learn the specifics. She came back and said that speaking as a lawyer *and* longtime friend of the family, if we want to close our doors, we can't do it under better terms."

"Is this about Sebastian Andrews?" Lily demands. "Oh my God! That's why he was hanging around all the time. To wear you down so you'd stop seeing him as the enemy."

"This isn't about Sebastian. I haven't seen him in weeks. Not since the cooking class."

I don't tell them that the fact that I haven't heard from him has led me to the same conclusion Lily's reached—that perhaps he was sticking around not because of any interest in me as a person, but to soften my perception of him so the offer on the table was no longer coming from an enemy, but . . . a friend?

If that was the case, he must have had a crisis of conscience, because he hasn't been around the shop, and maybe that's just as well. Maybe it's the same reason I had Bubbles & More's lawyer take care of all official correspondence. I may know in my heart that it's the right path, but it doesn't mean my heart doesn't also hurt that I couldn't make Bubbles work for the sake of my dad's memory—that I couldn't learn to love it like my parents did.

The whimsical part of me, the one that sings to pigeons, wants to keep my memories of Sebastian Andrews as far away from that pain as possible.

Caleb takes a sip of his sparkling water, stares at the can a moment, as though surprised to see it there, then sets it aside and looks back at the camera. "Okay, I'm just going to come out and say it. This is sort of an about-face from where we were a month ago. Maybe if we had Alec look over the numbers—"

"I did," Alec interjects. "Gracie's correct about the state of the store's finances."

He takes his wife's hand as he says it, and Lily glances over, blinking away tears. Even in my melancholy mood, I feel a warm feeling in my chest at the silent spousal connection that's both sweet and envy inducing.

When my sister turns back to the computer screen, her blue eyes have taken on a warrior's glint. "This is on me and Caleb. We didn't give you the support you need, Gracie, and the help we did provide was too little and too late. That ends now. Caleb, the new website looks great—I'm assuming you can add an e-commerce component, right? We can research what it takes to ship to different states—we can be the *country's* champagne resource, not just Midtown's. It'll be expensive to move into that space, but we can get a loan, we can grow the team—"

"Lil." I interrupt her softly and take the hand Alec's not holding, squeezing gently. I wait for her to look back at me, then speak the truth that's been quietly building inside me for weeks. Maybe longer. "I don't want that."

She blinks. "What do you mean?"

"I realize closing the store can't be a unilateral decision. If you want to keep it open, I'm happy to hand over the reins, but I need to step back. I *want* to step back."

"But you love Bubbles," Caleb protests. "It's always been your and Dad's thing—"

"It was *Dad's* thing," I clarify, firmly but gently. "It was never mine. I stepped in only because it was so important to Dad that it stay open, and in the family, and I realized it was going to be me or no one."

"Gracie, why didn't you tell us?" My sister looks stricken.

"I should have," I say. "Though I'm not sure I ever really admitted it to myself until recently. I don't blame you. Either of you." I look at Caleb. "But I also can't keep living for Dad, or for you guys. I have to live for me."

"I respect that," Caleb says quietly. "Though I still get to feel like an ass for acting like a baby about keeping the store open, when I didn't do much at all to help."

"Same," Lily says. She inhales and holds her breath for a second. "The deal is good?" She looks at me again.

"It's fair," I say. "And it provides severance for the staff, which is most important to me."

She nods. "Okay. I trust you."

"Me too," Caleb says, then looks at me and grins. "But now I'm dying to know . . . what will you do?"

"I have no idea," I say honestly. "But the severance will give me a bit of a buffer to figure it out."

Everyone nods, but there's a lingering silence that hangs in the air. Not awkward, not angry. Just a little bit sad as we all come to grips with what lies ahead. I thought I'd made peace with my dad's passing, but this feels a bit like saying goodbye to him all over again.

Lily is the first to break the silence. "So, we're doing this?"

"Just tell me where to sign," Caleb says. His smile slips. "Damn. It's sad though, isn't it? End of an era."

"No, no, no," Lily says, waving her hands. "We're not going to think like that. This is the right thing to do, and deep down, we all know it."

She's right. I *do* know it. And so I let my family try to distract me from the fact that I'm about to be unemployed with pizza and wine. I continue to badger my brother about meeting his girlfriend.

I smile. I laugh.

When I leave my sister's place, I feel the lightest I've felt in years.

And then I get on the subway and see the latest message from Sir.

My dear Lady,

First, my apologies for the delayed response. Out of respect for everything you are to me, I wanted to give your suggestion the consideration it deserves.

I'm tempted. You have no idea how tempted, how long I've wondered what you look like, what it would be like to hear your voice, to see your face as we talk about nothing. And everything.

But it's with immense regret—if nothing else, *please* believe my regret—that I must decline your offer. Not for always, but for now, the time isn't right for me to introduce a new variable into my life.

Please understand. Please.

I hope we might continue on as we have been. If not, if you're looking for something else, something more . . . I'll understand.

Yours in regret,

Sir

———————

To Sir, with reassurances,

Please don't think a thing of it. Of course we can go on as we've been! Here, I'll get us started. An important topic I find it hard to believe we haven't discussed yet: reality TV. Is there anything better? The drama? The suspense? The sheer juiciness of it all . . .

Lady

———————

My dear Lady,

Oh GOD.

Yours in dissent,

Sir

Seventeen

I don't want to say I've hit rock bottom. That would imply I'm at home in my PJs, digging into another pint of pistachio gelato, with no bra and hair that hasn't encountered shampoo in quite some time.

I'm fine. I am. My brain is very sure of this.

Sir is just some guy whose face I've never seen. Sebastian is just some businessman whose interest in me was purely financially motivated. I never had either of them, so I haven't lost either of them.

So why does my heart hurt?

There is a bittersweet silver lining to my personal life crashing and burning. My professional life is also crashing and burning, but at least I'm in the driver's seat there. With every longtime customer I've said goodbye to, with every discount sign I've hung, with every box of champagne I've carefully packaged to sell to one of the vendors who've been buying out our inventory, I feel a little more sure that this is *right*.

Scary. And sad. But I feel in my bones that this sharp turn in my life's path is the right one.

I smile at a young forty-something couple as I hand them

a crisp white paper bag. They're celebrating her one-year anniversary of being cancer-free and were thrilled when I pointed them to a particularly nice steal on our going-out-of-business table. A few of our nearby competitors bought out full and half cases, but for the one-off bottles, I've decided on an "everything must go" approach.

Dad's probably ticked about it from up in Heaven. While he himself was a coupon-cutting, deal-hunting aficionado—he loved himself a cheap Chianti—he and my mom had defined Bubbles as a luxury shop from the very beginning. *You don't see a sales rack at Cartier, do you, Gracie?*

In truth, I'd never set foot in Cartier. I *still* haven't, so I don't know what it's like.

But here's what I do know: The smile on that couple's face when I'd handed them a bottle of wine to celebrate being alive? The tears in the eyes of a grandmother buying champagne to celebrate her first grandson and finding something in her price range? *Worth it*, despite the loss. Which tells me something I've maybe known all along: I'd rather be a good person than a great businesswoman.

Of course, that's easy to say now that I have the financial buffer of the Andrews Corporation deal. Not that I'm set for life or anything. But for the first time *ever*, I've got a bit of breathing room in my budget. No more losing sleep about making sure I have enough to pay rent at home and the store. No more Groundhog Day resentment that I have to work seven days a week because I can't afford to bring on another employee. No more endless stress about being able to keep the employees I *do* have.

That, apart from our legacy coming to an end, has been one of the hardest parts of all this. Breaking the news to May, Josh, and Robyn that while they'd get six months' worth of pay, they'd need to find another job. That they'd all received the news with understanding and kindness had been a little bright spot in an otherwise bittersweet period of my life.

May in particular had been in favor of the decision. *Time to move on, in more ways than one.*

I know she was talking about letting go of my dad. I know that most of the reason she's stuck around the store is for me, but I also know a little part of it's for her—a way to stay connected with my father. I don't want that for her. To stay connected with his memory? Of course. I know she'll always love him. But I also want her to find that same happiness with someone else.

Robyn had been disappointed, but not surprised. In fact, she'd already started job hunting with the anticipation of the store closing, and I'm glad for it. She's smart, she's talented, and I'm confident she'll find someone or somewhere that can make use of those talents.

Strangely, it had been Josh whom I'd been dreading telling the most. I hate that he worked so darn hard to learn wine, to learn the shop . . . for nothing.

Not nothing, boss. I was a part of something good. No regrets.

Ironic. Ironic that the employee who's been a part of Bubbles's story for the shortest amount of time is the one who was able to sum it up the best. Part of something good indeed.

We'd celebrated that good thing last night with a farewell party here at the shop. Nothing big, nothing fancy. Just the staff, the Coopers sans Caleb, though he'd FaceTimed for a while, a few of our regulars, and close friends. Keva had shown up with Grady and trays of potato chip–crusted cheese and broccoli casserole in tow, which they'd insisted was the perfect pairing for the occasion. They'd been absolutely right.

A little part of me had wondered if Sebastian would show up unexpectedly, the way he had for all of our other events.

He had stayed away, and I'd told myself I was glad.

The party had been a blast—the perfect sendoff for thirty-nine years of serving champagne to Midtown. I'm glad we had it when we did, on the eve of the store closure, rather than after the doors had shuttered for good. It allowed me to show up for work today—for the last time—with the laughter and company of last night fresh in my mind. To somehow get through this day with a smile.

To get to this point. This moment.

Lily reaches out and squeezes my hand as we stand shoulder to shoulder staring at Bubbles's front door. Robyn and Josh are already gone for the day—no, for *good*. Behind me, I hear May chattering under her breath, trying to find her lipstick in her purse. Alec's around too, a calm, reassuring presence.

"You want me to do it?" Lily asks gently when I don't move.

I shake my head. "No, no. I just . . ." I squeeze my eyes shut. "Would it be okay . . . would you mind if I did this part alone? I think I need some time, just me and the store."

She squeezes my hand again. "Of course."

"Are you sure? This is your place too—"

"No," she says softly. "It hasn't been my place for a long time. And it never was, not like it was yours. Nobody should have to end a long-term relationship with an audience." Lily turns around to May and Alec. "Pack up, guys. We're headed out."

May pulls her lipstick out of her purse with triumph. "Just as soon as I'm dressed . . ."

She adds a thick layer of bright magenta and makes a kissing noise in my direction, then drops the lipstick back into her purse to get lost again—why she doesn't keep it in a side pocket, I have no idea. She picks up her bright purple trench coat and bag and comes toward me.

"You enjoy your alone time, love, but you need someone to cry on, you come by my place, okay?"

I smile and nod, not really trusting my voice at the moment. She puts both hands on my cheeks, her usual warrior expression unusually soft. "He's proud of you," she whispers. "Your mama too. They'd want you to choose *you*."

I manage another nod, my eyes watering this time, and she pulls me forward, pressing a kiss against my forehead. "Remember. My place if you need it. We'll get drunk, order cheese fries, and watch Katharine Hepburn movies."

She turns to leave, and as I've been doing all day, I try not to think about the fact that I'll never see her walk through that door again.

Lily and Alec approach me next. Together, but not, and I don't have the emotional energy to deal with that right now. So I let them hug me. I see Lily's eyes water and lift a finger. "Don't. We can't do that."

"Right, I know." She sniffles.

Alec pulls me in for a last hug, then kisses my cheek. He doesn't tell me he's there if I need him, but I know. I know they both are.

He holds the door for Lily, who starts to exit, then pauses in the doorway and turns, her eyes taking in the empty shelves. The last remaining boxes I need to pack. Alec and I don't move or speak, letting her say her farewells, not just to the shop, but to a stage of her life—our lives—now closed.

She nods once, mostly to herself, and steps out into the fall evening air. Alec gives me one last smile, then follows his wife out. Through the window I see him reach hesitantly for her hand. See her head snap up in surprise. See her fingers intertwine with his.

The simple, sweet gesture, one I've seen thousands of times over the years but not often enough lately, hits me right in the feels. And the emotions that have been teetering on a tightrope all day fall.

It's not a sob fest. Just a constant stream of quiet tears that I don't even fully register until the teardrops dangling off my jawline start to tickle. I wipe at them, but they keep coming.

With a quiet sob, I step forward and reach for the We're Open sign shaped like a champagne bottle.

I take a deep breath. I flip it.

Sorry! We're Closed!

Forever.

The plywood sways gently on its white string for just a second longer and then stills. I stay still too, letting myself be frozen in this moment.

And I realize my mistake.

I don't want to be alone.

I don't want to be alone, yet neither do I want to eat cheese fries with May or girl-talk with Keva or Rachel. I don't want to FaceTime my brother or even talk about the good old days with my sister.

I close my eyes and let myself want . . . *him*.

I want my musician with his long hair and brown eyes to take me into his arms and hold me. Or just make me laugh. Or let me talk about Dad. Or tell me everything's going to be okay.

And yet, something's not quite right. The daydream I've conjured up for so long, the face of my dream man has changed. He's a little bit taller, his hair a little darker.

His eyes aqua instead of brown.

"Damn it." No way am I letting Sebastian all up into this moment. This is my moment, and I know just how to celebrate. I pivot on my heel and head to the nearly empty cave to retrieve my bottle of Krug. I say *my* bottle of Krug, because Dad had bought each of us one on our twenty-first birthday. Not the Dom we'd opened on our birthday—the *ready to drink now* wine. But a *save for the right time* champagne.

Lily's had been on her wedding night. Caleb had opened his the night the Cubs won the World Series, because somehow the born-and-raised New Yorker has always had an obsession with a Chicago baseball team.

But I've been saving mine. I thought maybe it was for my wedding or the birth of my first child, but I realized just recently that this is the moment. A celebration. And a goodbye.

On a whim, because it feels right, I message Sir.

To Sir—you there?

I tuck the phone into the back pocket of my jeans as I pull out the bottle from its spot in the fridge and peel off the hot pink sticky note that reads *Gracie's—Don't Touch!*

I smile as I trace the ornate label, remembering my dad's proud announcement of exactly how expensive it was. I kiss my finger, press it to the label, then look up. "I love you, Dad."

There's no boom from the heavens in response. That's okay. Like May said, I have to believe my parents would support this decision.

There's no response from Sir either. That one stings a bit more.

I take out two tulip flutes—my favorite, and ones I deliberately hadn't packed away yet. I don't need both, but I figure it's a little more respectable to drink alone if you at least pretend there's another person in the room.

I stare at my phone, willing it to buzz with a notification from MysteryMate. Nothing.

My heart sinks a little, but I visualize throwing my heart a rope and tugging it back up again.

"Just one more thing in my life that's not going quite according to the fairy tale," I say quietly, reaching for the bottle and beginning to twist the wire cage. I remove it and the foil. I check my phone one last time for a message that isn't there.

Fine. It's *fiiiiine*. I close the app and bring up another sort of male companionship. More reliable. Michael Bublé's *Call Me Irresponsible* album is one of my favorites, and I play it now, the store so quiet in its emptiness that my little iPhone speaker seems to fill the space with Bublé's baritone.

Bublé reassures me that the best is yet to come, and I believe him. Perhaps more important, I decide to take action. I open the MysteryMate app again, only this time it's to scroll through new matches—something, I'm embarrassed to say, I haven't done in months.

For all my talk about wanting to find The One, I sure haven't been trying very hard.

I pick up the bottle of Krug and wrap my hands to twist off the cork the way I have thousands of times.

But the pop sounds wrong.

Because it *isn't* a pop.

I frown as I realize it's a knock at the door—a brisk, businesslike rap.

Lily. I've always wanted us to have that magical connection that twins have, at least in TV shows, and maybe I'm finally getting my wish. She must have sensed I didn't want to be alone after all, and—

I'm halfway to the door when I see through the window, even in the dark, that it's not Lily. It's not a woman at all.

The sight of a male silhouette outside the door while I'm in here alone should cause my pulse to race, and it does.

But not with fear. With something else.

I *know* this silhouette.

I move slowly, not sure how I feel about his presence. By the time I get to the door, I still haven't figured it out, but I unlock it anyway.

And open the door to Sebastian Andrews.

Eighteen

"What are you doing here?"

Sebastian rubs a hand over the back of his head and looks down at the ground. His other hand holds a cheap white plastic bag.

When he glances up, it's with a slight frown. "I don't know."

I lean against the door jamb. "You don't know what you're doing outside an out-of-business wine shop at 10:30 p.m.?"

Without looking, I flick my fingernail at the champagne sign. "We're closed. For good. Oh wait, you know that."

Sebastian exhales. "I'm probably the last person you want to see. It's inappropriate that I'm here given the circumstances. I just . . ."

He hands me the bag. "Lamb gyro. Just in case."

"Just in case?" I ask, taking the bag, but not bothering to hide my confusion.

Sebastian frowns again. "I don't know quite how to explain it. I just had the strangest sense . . ." His gaze finds mine. "That you needed something."

My smile slips. Here I'd been willing Sir to magically sense

I needed to talk. Or Lily to have some new surge of sibling connection. I'd been sending vibes out into the universe all right, and the person who'd felt them was . . . Sebastian Andrews?

"Anyway," he clears his throat, looking embarrassed. "I'll leave you to your . . ." He looks behind me, apparently noticing the empty store for the first time, and he looks regretful. And maybe a tiny bit guilty.

Again, those aqua eyes find mine, and again, I feel an annoying tug in my stomach.

"Are you okay?" he asks gently.

I make a rueful face and scratch my cheek. "My face is all blotchy, huh?"

"My mother would kill me if I answered that," he says with a slight smile. He reaches toward my face. His hand pauses, and when I don't move away, his thumb comes to rest against the center of my forehead in a gesture that's both surprising and . . . tender.

He swipes with his thumb, and when he pulls it back and shows me the pad of his finger, it's bright pink.

"Oh for God's sake," I mutter, rubbing at my forehead with the back of my hand. "May and her lipstick. I don't suppose you're old-fashioned and have a handkerchief tucked into your suit pocket there?"

"Normally, yes. But alas, I left it next to my pocket watch and top hat this morning."

I can't help the little sigh that slips out. "Don't you ever wish we could go back to that time? When men were gentlemen and ladies were . . . well actually, I guess we couldn't vote, huh?"

"Depends. Did men carry handkerchiefs and pocket watches after the Nineteenth Amendment was ratified? I'd like to think yes."

"Ugh, I'm not in the mood for you to be likable right now," I say without heat.

He smiles, and I'm tempted to smile back, even as I'm irrationally angry. At him, for being so appealing when he's hung up on some other woman. At me, for hating that other woman . . .

"Thanks for the food," I say, giving the bag a little jiggle. "But I have more work I should get back to, and I'm sure you've got some*one* to get back to."

The warmth in his eyes fades. I try to tell myself his expression is irritation or wounded pride. But it looks a lot like hurt.

Sebastian gives a single nod and takes a step backward. "Ah. Never let it be said I can't take my cue. Good night, Ms. Cooper."

He turns away, and the second he does, I know this is all wrong.

"Wait." I reach out and grab his sleeve. He's not wearing a coat over his suit jacket, and the crisp texture of the suit sleeve reminds me of the night he'd walked me home and lent me his jacket.

His teal eyes glance down at my hand, then back to my face. Questioning. Hoping?

I shift to the side and tilt my head. *Come in.*

He steps into the empty Bubbles, though it feels a lot less empty with him in it.

By now Bublé's moved on to singing about him and Mrs. Jones as I set the white bag on the counter.

Sebastian looks around the near-empty room, his expression betraying nothing, at least until he notes the champagne. The two glasses. "You were expecting company."

"Sort of. It's complicated," I say with a little smile.

"Ah." His voice is a touch sharp. "Your suitor."

"*Suitor.* I like that word." I pick up the champagne bottle and give it a twist, the sharp crack of the cork creating a pleasant sort of harmony with the old-school music. "I think I undersold that last time. Complicated doesn't even begin to cover the situation with my *suitor*."

"No?" he asks, coming to stand across from me at the counter. I pour the wine and glance up, expecting to see him taking note of the bottle's label, but instead he's watching me.

I let his question hang in the air. I don't want to think about Sir's rejection just now. In fact, I realize, it's strange how little I seem to be able to think about Sir in Sebastian's presence, or Sebastian while messaging with Sir. It's as though my brain's put up some sort of buffer that prevents me from comparing the two men.

Perhaps because my heart knows it would have to choose.

I finish pouring the glasses and hand one to Sebastian.

He hesitates. "You really want to be drinking champagne? With me? Tonight?"

"This is a strange little twist of fate, to be sure," I say, looking around at the empty store. Empty because of him. But because of me as well. "But fitting, wouldn't you say?" I lift my glass. "To Bubbles."

He lifts his as well. "To Bubbles. To new beginnings."

I nod, about to sip, but he adds one more. "To the unexpected."

Sebastian catches my eyes as he says it, our gazes holding as we click our glasses and sip. The wine is outstanding. And has nothing to do with the butterflies in my stomach. The dryness in my mouth. The slight fuzziness where logic should be.

"This is incredible," he says, finally seeming to register his beverage. He reaches for the bottle and blinks. "And very expensive."

I shrug. "For all my preaching to my customers—former customers—about treating every day like a special occasion, I guess I'm old school. I've been saving this particular bottle for an *extra*special occasion, bittersweet as it may be."

"And here you are, sharing it with a man you hate."

I quickly shake my head. "I don't hate anybody."

"Extreme dislike?" he asks with a grim smile.

I exhale. "Closing Bubbles was likely inevitable," I say softly. "But I won't claim that the constancy of your letters and your sheer persistence didn't shove me along. Perhaps before I was ready. Or perhaps I should be thanking you. I'm not quite sure, to be honest."

His gaze flickers with regret. "Ms. Cooper—"

I quickly shake my head. "I don't want to talk business, Mr. Andrews. Not tonight. That part is done. I had my attorney handle everything for a reason."

"What reason?"

"So I don't come to hate you," I say, giving him a quick grin.

He looks off-balance for a moment, then lets out a quiet

chuckle. "You did warn me during our first meeting that you share your every thought."

Not my every thought.

I pull a stool over and hop onto it. I point at the other stool, but he shakes his head. I shrug and reach for the lamb gyro, smiling a little as I realize I'm about to combine cheap New York street meat, extraordinarily expensive champagne, and Sebastian Andrews.

A strange blend that is surprisingly . . . perfect.

"Want to split this?" I ask, unwrapping it.

"I don't believe there's a knife."

I shrug and take a bite, then hand it to him. Sebastian hesitates only a second, looking vaguely nonplussed, as though sharing food is a novelty. Then he takes a bite—a large one that makes me think he skipped dinner or had a salad—and hands it back.

It's about as intimate a meal as I've had in recent memory, yet nothing about it feels weird.

"So," I say, taking a bite and wiping my chin. "How've you been?"

He takes the gyro and stares at it, though he's not really seeing it. "Fine."

I lift my eyebrows. "Uh-huh."

He still hasn't touched the gyro, so I take it back and take another bite.

"You could try it my way," I say with a grin. "A little more babble, a little less stoicism."

"All right," he says slowly. "You asked how I've been. I've been conflicted."

"Oh man," I say, lifting my champagne flute in a toast. "I hear that."

Sebastian apparently changes his mind about sitting, because he moves around the counter and pulls out the second stool after all. He drags it across the hardwood floor until it's across from me. He sits. Takes the gyro out of my hand.

"What are you conflicted about?" he asks.

"Nope. You started it. You go first."

He takes his time chewing and swallowing, his expression guarded when he meets my eyes again. "It's about a woman."

My stomach tightens in unmistakable jealously, which I remind myself is unfair.

I smile and shrug. "Mine is about a man. Maybe we can help each other."

His eyes flash for a minute before he exhales and nods. "I care about her. I think about her more than I should. In fact, I find I'm thinking about her almost always. And yet, recently when I've thought about taking the next step, moving forward, something stops me. As though the moment isn't right. Does that make sense?"

"Unfortunately, yes," I say ruefully, thinking of Sir's most recent message. "But you want my thoughts on the right moments in life?"

"You've got kind of an Amazonian warrior gleam in your eye, so I'm not really sure," he admits skeptically.

"Here's what I think," I proceed anyway, balling up my napkin and tossing it into the plastic bag. "I think relationships are a lot like champagne. This bottle here"—I lift it and pour us each a little more—"it's crazy expensive. My dad got all of us Cooper kids a vintage from the year we were born for our twenty-first birthdays and told us to save it for the *right time*. We always interpreted that as save it for a special occasion. Engagements. Weddings. Celebrations. Baseball, if you're my brother." I hold the neck of the bottle, study the label. "But my dad didn't say save it for a special occasion. He said save it for the *right time*. It's a crucial difference, I'm realizing."

"And this is your right time? Here? With me?" he asks, his voice rough.

"Apparently. And that's sort of my point." I set the bottle down and look at him. "I don't think you can *plan* for the right time. Or the right woman. As far as timing's concerned, maybe sometimes you've got to *make* it the right time and simply *trust* that it's the right woman."

He sets the gyro aside—it's a mangled mess now, and neither of us reaches for it again. "What if pursuing one path costs you another?"

"That, my dear sir, is what you call *life*."

I stiffen a little in shock at what I've just said. *My dear sir.*

I feel both instant remorse, as though I've betrayed everything that is most dear to me, and something else I can't explain—a fleeting sense that I've just *uncovered* everything that is most dear to me.

The sentiment disappears before I have a chance to fully decipher it, but most puzzling of all is the look on Sebastian's face, a near exact mirror of my own shock and discomfort, which makes no sense. He can't possibly know what that phrase means to me, unless . . .

My stunned brain runs through everything I know of

Sir, everything I know of Sebastian. Both men in Manhattan, which means nothing—there are millions of those. But there are other things. The fact that both were in relationships when we first met, but no longer are. That he'd ordered lemon sorbet that night in the park, the quick wit, the unexpected kindness. Most telling of all, my own reaction to both men . . .

My fleeting sense of wondrous hope evaporates almost immediately as I recall one crucial detail: I've met Sebastian Andrews's parents—Sir's father passed away.

Not the same man then. The disappointment at the realization is severe. It would have explained so much. How I could feel pulled to both of these men in the same urgent, inexplicable way. How I always feel guilty thinking about one while talking to the other. But most especially, it would have solved the biggest problem of all:

Choosing one would mean losing the other—a thought that feels nearly unbearable.

To cover my disappointment that they can't possibly be the same man, I force a smile and resume conversation as though nothing's happened.

"Anyway," I say lightly. "I could be wrong. But I've got to wonder if relationships, especially the complicated ones, the ones worth getting right . . . I wonder if they're not like fine wine. Maybe you're just supposed to *drink the damn thing*."

Sebastian smiles—a *real* smile that softens his hard features. "An interesting approach for a wine expert."

"*Former* wine expert. I'm out of that game, thanks to you." But there's no heat to it, and I bat my eyelashes a bit.

"Out of the game?" he says in surprise. "I assumed you'd stay in the business in some way."

I shake my head. "I don't think so. It was always my dad's dream. Not mine."

"So what's next?"

"Well, I've got a few months to figure it out, also thanks to you. Which is a good thing, because I don't have a clue," I admit.

He studies me over the flute. "What about those dreams of being an artist."

I smile. "I think that ship has sailed in the same direction as your jockey ambitions."

"I disagree," he says. "I haven't so much as been near a horse in close to ten years. You're actively creating excellent art pieces."

I blink in surprise. "You knew?"

"That the paintings in the shop are yours? I had a hunch."

"How'd you figure it out?"

"Well, not because of your signature. What is it, a shoe?"

I smile a little and take another sip of champagne. "Yes. Cinderella's glass slipper. It was one of the first things I learned to draw. I was big into all things fairy tales. I started using it as my signature, which, when I was nine, felt extremely sneaky and clever. It sort of stuck."

I tilt my head curiously. "But really, how'd you know they were mine? I don't tell many people."

He shrugs. "I'm not sure. I've suspected, I think, for a while. The look on your face when I called them cutesy. It was more than professional pride. It was personal. Then, when you mentioned that night at the park that you wanted to be an artist, it sort of confirmed it."

I lift my fingers in a little salute. "Hats off, Sherlock."

He shifts a bit on the stool and waits until I look back at him. Which I do, warily.

"They're good," he says. "The paintings."

I roll my eyes. "He says, after realizing he put his foot in his mouth earlier with the *Cutesy Tinker Bell* comments."

"They're *good*." His voice is firm. Warm. Confident.

I want to accuse him of groveling, of trying to save face or digging himself out of the hole he dug, but he doesn't speak like a man trying to gain ground or backpedal. He sounds like a man speaking the truth.

And it means a lot. To have someone who's not related, who's not a friend, compliment my work.

I wipe an imaginary bit of nothing away from my mouth to do something with my hands, then finally gather the courage to look at him. To *really* look at him, because he's looking right at me.

"Thank you." My voice is quiet. Not a whisper, but close.

"You're welcome." His voice is quiet too, and for a moment, his gaze drops to my mouth.

He finishes the rest of his glass with a large swallow that probably has my dad rolling in his grave. "I should probably go. Let you finish up here."

"Sure, yeah. Thanks for the food. Your spidey sense was right. I did need it."

Or maybe I needed you.

I shove that thought away.

"Thanks for sharing your *right moment* champagne with a guy who put you out of business."

"What can I say, I guess I'm a sucker for irony," I say with a little smile, unlocking the door to let him out.

"Yes," he sounds distracted as he steps outside, but then he turns back at the last minute so we're standing nearly toe to toe, and I have to tilt my head all the way back to look at him.

"This guy of yours, the complicated one," he says, eyes latching on to mine. "He's *the* one?"

My breath catches at the question. I want to look away, but his eyes seem to hold me still. "I don't know," I admit quietly, to myself for the first time. "I thought so, but now . . . I'm not so sure."

His eyes gleam with something that looks like satisfaction, and his response knocks everything inside me off balance.

"Good."

Nineteen

"I still can't believe you came. And you didn't tell me," I say, hugging my little brother for what's probably the hundredth time since he knocked on the front door of Bubbles—or what *was* Bubbles—earlier that afternoon.

"What can I say, I thrive on surprises," Caleb says, picking up the box I slide across the counter and carrying it to the small stack near the front door.

It's two days after we closed, two days after my night, or whatever that was, with Sebastian. Technically, we have the space for a couple of more days—through the end of the month. But now that we're done, I'm ready to be . . . *done*.

After doing a walk-through with an uptight Andrews Corporation woman in a pantsuit and a severe bun, I just needed to gather the last odds and ends and check the drawers for forgotten items—where I've found four of May's earrings, one of which I'm fairly sure is a testicle.

I was holding it when my brother walked through the front door, and he confirmed, 100 percent: testicle.

"What's left?" he asks.

"Just the fridge," I say, nodding toward the cave. "I don't

even know if it's ours or if it came with the building. It's just always been there."

"Anything in it?"

I shrug. "A couple of beers. I'm not sure where they came from."

He strolls toward the door to the cave, in his work boots and faded jeans and a long-sleeve green Henley. He returns with two bottles of beer and uses the side of the counter to expertly pop the caps off.

"Can we drink beer in a champagne shop?" I whisper.

"Dad?" Caleb says, glancing toward the ceiling. "Mom?"

He looks over at me with a rueful expression. "Damn. They said it's not appropriate."

Then he hands me one and clinks the neck to mine before taking a long drink.

I smile. "I thought our parents said no?"

"They're parents. They're supposed to say no, and we kids are supposed to do the opposite of whatever they say."

"I don't think that's how it works."

He leans his elbows on the counter. "That's because you never went through a rebellious stage. Lily either."

"You went through enough for the three of us."

"You're welcome. Drink your beer. It's the champagne of the people."

"Is that a saying in New Hampshire?" I take a sip of the beer. Not my favorite, but not bad.

"Nope, just a fact. Lily text you back about dinner?"

I pick up my phone. "She did. She made reservations at some place in the West Village for seven thirty. She also sent about four other texts regarding your disregard for schedules and your lack of concern for other people's lives. Also, she's excited to see you. And she said not to tell you she cried when I told her you were in town."

He smiles but looks a little guilty. "Damn. I didn't realize I was the pillar of the family."

"Hardly. We just miss you. A lot. And I'm not lecturing." I lift my hand to reassure him. "But you did basically vanish into the night. We barely had a chance to register you were leaving, and then you were . . . gone."

"Yeah. I'm not proud of that," he says on an exhale. "Amanda gave me hell when I told her that story."

"Ah yes. The girlfriend I'm not allowed to talk about."

"You're allowed to talk about her, just not *to* her."

"Hey, for the record, I think it's completely normal for older sisters to go through their little brother's phones looking for their new girlfriend's number."

"For the record, it's completely not. Do I harass you about your love life?"

"No. You never even ask."

He wrinkles his nose. "Do you want me to ask?"

"I want you to care," I say a little quietly, pulling at the corner of the beer bottle label.

Caleb puts down his beer with a thunk and straightens. "You did not just say that."

I laugh. "I know, I know. You care."

"I care. I care a hell of a lot. I just don't *really* want to know who you're boning unless he's a creep I need to beat up." He narrows his eyes. "Is he?"

"No. Mostly because I'm not boning anyone."

"Thank God."

We sip our beers in silence for a second, and I look up. "We never did really talk about it though. Why you moved, I mean."

He sighs. "To be honest, it was something I'd wanted to do for a while. I like New York fine, but I don't love it the way you and Lily do. Even as a kid, I only ever wanted to go camping on spring break, remember?"

"I do. And when you got your way, it was *the worst*."

Caleb smiles. "Anyway, I mentioned it to Dad once—just that I was thinking about it—and I got some big lecture about family and loyalty and how he wasn't going to be around forever . . ."

"He did give a mean guilt trip," I say.

"Totally." Caleb looks thoughtful. "That why you took over the shop? Guilt trip?"

"A little, I suppose. I take responsibility for my decisions though. On some level I must have wanted to run Bubbles."

Or was too scared to pursue something that might matter more.

"I still feel like a shit for leaving it to you, all while making a bunch of noise about keeping the family business alive."

"Water, bridge," I say, making a sweeping motion with my beer bottle. "I'm just happy you're happy. I'm hoping to get in on some of that myself."

There's a knock at the door, and since I haven't bothered to lock it, someone walks in.

"Oh, I'm sorry," I call out. "We're no longer open for business."

"Yeah, I'm sure the completely empty space didn't spell that out," Caleb says.

I swat his head as I pass by to see who's just entered the shop, thinking it might be a lost tourist or a former customer who didn't get the memo.

It's neither. A man I don't recognize is studying the empty space with a curious, assessing eye, and he continues to stroll around the room as though he's supposed to be there.

"May I help you?" I ask.

He turns, and I'm certain I've never met him. He's tall and reed thin, with a receding hairline, wire-frame glasses, and an intensity that's not aggressive or unfriendly, but very purposeful.

He tilts his head, brown eyes looking at me for a long moment. "Gracie Cooper?"

"Yes? Do I know you?"

"About to," he says, reaching into the jacket of his purple tweed blazer over a black turtleneck and coming out with a deep purple business card.

"Hugh Wheeler," he says as he hands it over.

I look down at the card, which has his name and beneath it the words Wheeler Art Gallery. I'm not familiar with it, but the address indicates it's in Chelsea.

"Have we met? If you're looking for champagne, I'm no longer in that business, but I'd be happy to give you the name—"

"No, thank you. My husband and I visit the Champagne region every spring and rent a wine locker in West SoHo specifically to store it."

"That's great." I smile. "So, what can I help you with?"

"I'd like to see your art."

My smile freezes. "I'm sorry?"

"You're an artist," he says.

"I . . . no. I mean, I paint sometimes, but . . . how did you know that?"

"I like to call them spies, though I suppose *sources* is the socially appropriate term."

He pulls out his cell phone, taps it, then turns it around so I'm looking at a photo of my art corner here in the store before I took everything down.

"Is that your work?"

My head is spinning. "Yes, but—"

"Do you have any here?" He looks around, disappointment plain on his face as he takes in the blank walls, the empty shelves.

"No—"

"Yes she does," Caleb says, coming up behind me. He reaches out a hand toward Hugh, who looks torn between dismay at Caleb's less than urbane clothing and admiration for his obvious good looks.

"Did you forget, sis?" he says, grinning down at me, unabashed. "This big thing over here by the door. You lectured me not to bend it because it had your *art* in it." He gives me a wide grin as he easily tears open the packing tape.

"Caleb," I say in a warning voice.

The mysterious Hugh Wheeler is already pulling out the pieces. There are only three there. Two that didn't sell, and one—of the man with the aqua eyes—that I never put out on the floor.

Hugh pulls them all out and lines them against the front

window, staring down at them for what must be half my life span, not moving, not making a sound.

Even Caleb starts to look a little unsure, and I have to bite my tongue not to say, *See, this is why I didn't want to show him; I'd rather not know if I have no talent.*

Hugh slowly turns toward me. "I like these. They make me smile."

Caleb lets out a laugh but quickly hides it behind a cough. This man hasn't produced anything close to a smile since he walked through the door. Still, he's not unfriendly. Just a little awkward and intense.

"Um. Thank you?" I say.

"Do you have more?" he asks.

"One more finished at home. Another in progress."

He nods. "Good. If you can pull together at least ten—twenty is better—I'd like to discuss the possibility of showing your work in my gallery."

"I—what? My work's just for fun, it's not . . . art gallery."

"Maybe not all art galleries. Not the pretentious ones that think it's only art if it looks like a blob and requires a PhD to decipher. But I show art that people *like*. That they want on their walls, that they want to give their friends. Specifically, art that people will *buy*."

He reaches out and flicks the card in my hand. "Text me when the pieces are done. Don't call. I won't pick up, and I never check voice mail."

Stunned, I manage a nod, and Hugh moves toward the door—I say moves, not walks, because he just sort of whispers along like the wind.

Hugh pauses one last time and looks down at the paintings. "Your signature. What is that?"

"Oh, it's a shoe. Glass slipper. You know . . . Cinderella. I was sort of a fairy tale nut when I was younger."

Caleb gives me an *oh come on . . . when you were younger?* look that Hugh either ignores or misses, because he's still looking at the paintings.

"Huh." He stares a moment longer, and this time when he looks back at me, there's an actual smile on his face. "Guess that makes me your fairy godmother."

I get the feeling that if he had a wand, he'd use it. Instead, he winks, then he's gone.

"Well, well. Looks like your fairy tale's the real deal after all," my brother says as the door clicks closed.

I don't respond.

I'm too busy trying to figure out what the hell just happened.

twenty

"You need to order more razor blades!"

I look up from the palette where I've been trying to get the exact right shade of green I have in my mind's eye, but the darn thing keeps skewing toward mint when I want moss. "What?"

My brother sticks his head out of my bathroom door, lower face covered in shaving cream. He holds up my pink razor. "I just put on your last fresh blade. You'll need to order more."

"Use your own razor!"

"Forgot it." He pops back into the bathroom, and I shake my head and go back to my mixing.

I love Caleb, and I'm glad he's staying with me while he's in town. I'm also a *little* glad that he's spending his last night before going back to New Hampshire with his friends.

"Where are you guys headed?" I ask.

"Some new bar down in the East Village. Fred's girlfriend's the bartender, so hopefully we'll get a few drinks out of it." I hear the swish of water in the sink. "You sure don't want to come?"

"Positive," I say as he comes out of the bathroom with a towel in hand, drying his face. "Also, put on some clothes."

"Adrian will be there," he says, looping the towel around his neck and tugging on both ends.

"Who?" I ask distractedly.

"My friend Adrian. He thinks you're cute. Come with. Meet him. It could be good for you."

I look up. "Good for me how?"

He sighs. "Sis. I'm thrilled that the art thing is happening for you. But you've barely left the apartment in days, you've only talked to me and Keva, and Lily told me that the closest thing you've had to a boyfriend is some dude you've never met who probably collects hair."

"He does not collect hair," I say. "And I knew it was a mistake to send you and Lily to lunch without supervision."

Turning away, I swatch the paint on my test canvas. Mossy green. Perfect for the springtime Central Park picnic piece I've sketched out.

"G," Caleb says a bit impatiently.

I glance over and see his look of concern. "What?"

He sighs. "I can't believe I'm saying this, but I miss the old Gracie—the one who always thought true love was just around the corner."

I set my brush down. "Hold on. Are you calling me cynical?"

He purses his lips. "I'm saying that it's going to be awfully hard to find that Prince Charming you always used to talk about if you don't even try."

I heave out a sigh. "Okay. You're right. You are. But I'm really on a roll here, and this thing with Hugh Wheeler feels like a once-in-a-lifetime opportunity. So how about this: I rain check tonight but promise to go out with your friend Adrian some other time."

"Deal," Caleb says, and I feel instant regret.

I don't want to go out with some random guy. I want . . .

A knock at the door scatters my thoughts.

"It's probably Keva," I tell Caleb, turning back to my painting. "Can you let her in?"

My brother opens the door, and there's a pause.

"Um, hello. I'm looking for Gracie Cooper?"

I whirl around from my easel at the masculine voice. One I never expected to hear at my front door.

"And you are?" Caleb asks, his tone protective.

I set my paint brush aside and wipe my hand on my smock as I walk toward the door. "Caleb, this is Sebastian Andrews."

"The dude who put Bubbles out of business?"

Sebastian flinches. Almost imperceptibly, but it's there.

"Hi," I say. Is my voice breathless? Crap. My brother is still blocking the door, and I shove him aside.

"I didn't mean to interrupt your evening," Sebastian says a little stiffly.

"Really?" Caleb says. "What would you call dropping by unannounced at seven o'clock on a Friday?"

"Oh my God," I mutter, pushing him toward the bathroom. "Go get dressed."

Caleb gives Sebastian one last warning look, followed by a *what the hell?* glance in my direction.

I ignore it. Mainly because I don't have a clue what Sebastian Andrews is doing at my front door.

"Come on in," I say, standing to the side.

He shakes his head. "I don't want to interrupt your . . . date."

I blink. My what now? *Gross.*

Then I see the scene from his eyes—a half-naked man with a proprietary glower has just answered my front door.

I tilt my head in the direction of Caleb as he comes out of the bathroom, the towel thankfully replaced with jeans and a blue checked dress shirt. "My brother. He's staying with me a few days while he's in town."

Sebastian's aqua eyes snap to Caleb, his expression showing a blink-and-you-miss-it flicker of . . . relief?

"Nice to meet you," Sebastian says.

"Uh-huh." My brother is buttoning the cuff of his sleeve, still scowling.

"Caleb," I say on a sigh. "Be polite."

"Compared to our first meeting," Sebastian says to me, "I'd say this is an improvement."

"Hey! I was polite."

Sebastian lifts an eyebrow. *Were you?*

Caleb's scowl has lessened considerably as he gives Sebastian and me a curious look. "Nice to put a face with the name," Caleb says to Sebastian.

"Which I imagine frequently goes hand in hand with profanity?"

My brother grins as he steps out into the hallway. "I'll never tell. See you later. G, I'll probably be late. I'll try to be quiet if *you* remind your cat I've called dibs on the couch."

"You're never quiet," I grumble.

"Be good," Caleb calls as he jogs down the stairs. "Don't forget about the cat."

"Sorry about him," I say, shutting the door.

Sebastian's scanning my tiny, slightly messy apartment curiously, focusing on my in-progress painting before turning back to me. He must have come straight from the office, because as usual, he's wearing a suit. Dark charcoal this time, with a dark purple tie.

I start with the most pressing question.

"How do you know where I live?"

"I walked you home that night after Central Park, remember?"

"I do." *Too well.* "But you left me at the front door, how do you know which unit I lived in?"

He scratches just behind his ear, looking slightly guilty. "We have your info in the system. I broke company policy, and probably a few laws, by looking it up."

"Why?" I ask plainly.

He reaches into the inner pocket of his suit jacket and pulls out an envelope. "I wanted to give you this. Normally we'd mail it, but . . ."

He shrugs, looking embarrassed.

I take the envelope, noting the now-familiar logo of his family's company. I don't open it. Raising my eyes, I look him straight in the eye. "Last time I got an envelope from you that looked like this, my life turned upside down."

To his credit, he doesn't look away. "I know."

The straightforward honesty catches me off guard. Who am I kidding, this entire situation has caught me off guard.

He's close enough that I can see his eyelashes—black and spiky, the exact color of his five o'clock shadow.

Unsettled, I glance down, then use the envelope as an excuse to turn away slightly, my thumb sliding under the flap. There's a check inside.

"Wow," I say after a moment, staring down at it. "That is . . . a lot of money."

"It's the agreed-upon amount," he says quietly.

I knew it was coming. And of course, it's not all mine. It's made out to the business. But still. *Holy crap.*

I give Sebastian a wry smile. "I'm guessing my very humble abode reaffirms your suspicion that I needed this money sooner rather than later."

I expect him to look around my apartment, note its small size, the tired couch, the outdated kitchen. Instead, he holds my gaze. "That's not why I came."

My breath catches. "No? Then why?"

His aqua eyes lock on mine a second longer before he steps around me and goes to the easel. He studies it for a long minute.

He looks back at me. "It didn't occur to me that you used pencil first."

"I don't always," I say, sliding the check back into the envelope and setting it on the kitchen table. "And when I do, it's usually only on a practice run, not the final."

"How many versions of each painting do you do?"

"Usually not more than two unless I goof up. But I almost always plan out what I'm going to do in my sketchbook before it makes it to this stage."

"What's this one?" he asks, leaning forward to look closer. My pencil strokes are light, more guidelines than actual sketch.

"Central Park. A picnic. I haven't decided yet if it'll be a couple or a family. Maybe a girls' day or just a lone woman reading with her dog."

As though in protest at the word *dog*, Cannoli comes strolling out from wherever he's been hiding with a long meow and hops up onto the arm of the couch, tail twitching as he gives Sebastian what can only be described as a skeptical once-over.

The cat meows again, a little more friendly this time, and Sebastian steps toward him, extending a finger and rubbing the side of the cat's face. Cannoli's eyes close, and he pushes his entire head against Sebastian's hand, pressing his face into the large palm.

I'm not going to lie, it's pretty heart melting.

"Boy or girl?" he asks, still petting the cat.

"Boy. Cannoli."

He gives me a sharp look, and I shrug with a smile. "What? I like dessert."

His eyes narrow just slightly. "What's your favorite kind of dessert?"

"I'm not terribly picky. If it's sweet and delicious, I love it. Though I do think it's hard to beat really good ice cream."

"Gelato," he guesses, though it's more statement than question.

"Totally," I smile, thinking of Sir. "Give me a pint of pistachio gelato, and there's basically zero chance that I won't finish the entire thing. By myself. In one sitting."

He frowns. "That night in the park. We stopped at the ice cream truck, but you didn't get ice cream. You got lemon sorbet."

I smile, remembering. "A whim. A . . . friend of mine swears by it. I think it's an affront to dessert, but I realized I couldn't really say that when I hadn't given it a chance."

"What's the verdict?"

"I still think it's an affront to dessert," I say with a grin.

Sebastian doesn't grin back but studies me with a strange expression. Then I realize that he'd ordered lemon sorbet with me, and maybe I'd just insulted his dessert of choice. I shake my head. What is it with the men in my life liking frozen lemon nonsense?

Perhaps more important: When did I start counting Sebastian Andrews as a man in my life?

Cannoli grows bored and ambles off to my bedroom, and Sebastian nods toward the stack of finished paintings against the wall. "May I?"

"Um . . ." I hesitate, remembering the one of the man with the aqua eyes. It doesn't *look* like Sebastian. It doesn't look like anyone, really. It's more shadow than features. Still, those eyes . . .

"Sure," I say, because I can't think of a way to say no that wouldn't be rude.

I expect him to flip through them quickly, but he takes his time, holding each painting and studying it thoroughly before moving on to the next. I hold my breath when he gets to the one of the man.

He looks at it the same way he did the others, then sets it

aside without a word and moves onto the next, seemingly without noticing the unusual eye color. I slowly exhale.

Finally, he gets to the last one—there are eleven in that stack, the ones I think are my best, though I'm still working to get twenty I feel are good enough to take to Mr. Wheeler.

Sebastian turns around to face me once more. "They're charming, and no, I don't mean that to be the least bit condescending. Hugh's going to be thrilled."

"Thank you," I say, pleasure rushing over me. "I've been—wait . . . Hugh? Hugh Wheeler?"

He shrugs, then nods once.

I stare at him in confusion. "How did you know that a Chelsea art gallery was—"

Dismay settles low in my stomach as I realize there's only one way he'd know about Hugh Wheeler approaching me. "It was *you*."

Sebastian blinks, looking taken aback by the sharpness in my tone.

"*You* were his source," I say. "You were the one who told him how to find me."

"Yes, I went to school with his brother. He's a friend. I thought—"

"Oh my God." I dig my fingers into my hair and tug. "I'm one of your *projects*."

"My what?"

"Another Jesse. Another Avis. You all but told me that this is what you do—push people out of business and then fix them up with some other venture so you don't have to feel guilty. The new restaurant with Jesse. Setting Avis up in Florida.

With me, it's buying me lamb gyros, sucking up to my cat, and calling in a favor with a friend to get my art displayed. It's *pity*."

His eyes flash in anger. "That's not what's going on here."

I squeeze my eyes shut and press my thumbs against my eyelids as it all clicks into place. Every kind gesture, every moment, was merely him trying to assuage his conscience for his role in the failure of Bubbles.

I nod toward the kitchen table. "Did you bring Jesse and Avis their checks in person too?"

He says nothing.

"Did you?" I'm shouting now.

"Yes."

He says it calmly, and all of my shock and hurt fade into the background, replaced by aching disappointment. No, something a lot worse than disappointment.

Hurt. A hurt so deep it feels awfully close to heartbreak.

I let out a shaky laugh. "I can't believe I actually thought . . ." I shake my head.

He steps closer. "You thought what?" His voice is rough, his eyes seeming to plead with mine, and for an insane moment, I want to tell him.

I want to tell him to choose me, to feel about me the way I feel about him.

"Gracie—"

His use of my first name sends something warm curling through me, but I shove it aside.

"No." I shake my head. "I'm not going to stand here and become another one of your projects, another example you can rattle off to the next person you put out of business as proof that you're some sort of corporate savior who somehow improves people's lives when actually you ruin them—"

His eyes flash in anger. "What exactly have I *ruined*? I didn't put you out of business. I didn't sabotage your store. In fact, I *supported* your efforts. I showed up at your tasting and bought a case of sparkling wine. I showed up at your cooking class, paid full price. I'm being scorned, for what, exactly? For making a sound financial offer that *you* chose to accept? For mentioning your art to a friend? What's my crime here, Ms. Cooper?"

"I didn't need any of that! I didn't want it. I was *fine* before that day I ran into you on the sidewalk, before you showed up in my shop, before you stalked me at my house."

"*Stalked* you," he repeats. "Stalked you?" He stares at me a moment, then shakes his head. "Unbelievable."

Sebastian heads toward my front door, jerking it open, then turns back. "Don't worry, Ms. Cooper. This is the last you'll see or hear from me. Have a nice life."

The door slams shut as he walks out of my apartment. Out of my life.

I should feel relieved. Instead, I sit on my couch and cry.

To Sir, with a touch of melancholy,

I have a bit of a confession. I miss my dad every day—both my parents. Of course I do. But lately I'm a tiny bit glad that they passed on before seeing what a mess I've made of my life. Have you ever felt that with your dad? Relieved that he can't see you at your less than fine moments? Not that you have those, of course . . .

Lady

_____

My dear Lady,

Oh, I most definitely have those "less than fine" moments. More, I think, than I even realized until they've been recently pointed out to me. And while I wasn't close enough to my father to feel that same pang you're feeling, I do know there's no worse feeling than realizing you've hurt the last person on earth you would have wanted to.

Yours in shared regrets,

Sir

_____

Oh man, I so hear that. I've been reflecting on some of my childlike behavior in recent days. I've treated someone unkindly who, in hindsight, I'm not confident deserved it.

_____

There is plenty I don't know about you, to be sure. But I do know that you're kind.

twenty-One

Two days after my fight with Sebastian, Caleb's gone back to New Hampshire, and I find myself wanting the closest thing I have to a mother.

I don't call first. I should have, but . . . I didn't think.

It doesn't matter. May opens the door to me, takes one look at my limp ponytail, shadowed eyes, and mismatched clothes and brings me in for a long, tight hug that smells like rose perfume and comfort.

She draws back, studies my face, then points at the purple couch. "Sit. I'll make tea."

I do as she says, kicking off my shoes and pulling my knees up to my chin as I hear the quiet, soothing noises of the water, the kettle, mugs on the counter.

I hear her voice, not quite hushed, but deliberately quiet as she speaks on the phone. I wince as I realize she's rescheduling something.

"You had plans tonight," I say when she comes back into the living room carrying an old-fashioned tea tray. I'm already putting my shoes back on, but she shakes her head sternly.

"A date with a man with good hands," she says happily,

pouring the tea. "Who happens to be free tomorrow night, and more importantly, who understands the importance of family."

I don't drink tea very often, but May knows my coffee habits well enough to add two sugar cubes and a generous dash of cream before handing me the teacup.

"This is pretty," I say, tracing the delicate floral pattern on the rim of the saucer with my nail.

"My first love's grandmother gave it to us as a wedding gift. I don't use it often enough," she says, lifting the cup and gazing at it fondly. "I confess I've been committing the ultimate crime by keeping something so dear on a shelf rather than enjoying it. But," she says, taking a sip of the tea and setting it back on the table. Her earrings are ladybugs today, and they sway as she sits back in her chair. "You're not here to talk about my mistakes, are you?"

I wince. "So you think I've made mistakes?"

"I think *you* think you've made some."

I pull my knees up once more, resting the saucer carefully atop them as I stare down at the tea, which is more cream colored than tea colored, exactly as I like it.

May sips her tea in silence for a while, letting me gather my thoughts, and I'm grateful for it. As much as I adore my sister and my girlfriends, they're always so eager to help that they start offering advice before I even know what I'm asking.

"Okay, here's the thing," I say on an exhale, taking a sip of tea before setting the saucer carefully on the coffee table. I sit cross-legged, hands folded in my lap. "I feel *lost*. I used to wake up knowing what each day held. I used to know exactly what I wanted my life to look like—"

"And what was that?" May interjects. "Tell me old Gracie's vision."

"I was a successful shop owner," I say. "Not rich, but comfortable, with a steady influx of regular customers. I was married to a man who was friendly, approachable, good with the customers. We'd run Bubbles together, and in our off time, we'd embrace our hobbies. I'd paint. He'd write music, or whatever his passion was. We'd have children, and they'd do their homework at Bubbles just as I did . . ."

"It sounds nice," May says noncommittally.

I nod.

"It also sounds familiar . . ." she says thoughtfully, then snaps her fingers. "Oh yes. You're describing your father's life, and from what I understand, your late mother's as well. With one key difference."

"Times have changed, and niche champagne shops are no longer a viable business model?" I say glumly.

"No. The difference is that that was never *your* vision. You were trying to live his life, Gracie, and you weren't meant to."

"Maybe so," I admit. "But that doesn't change the fact that I seem to have a big gaping hole in my life now. I can barely piece together my present, much less my future."

"Why in God's name would you want to piece together your future?" May asks, sounding aghast. "Half the fun's in not knowing."

I let that soak in a little bit, then squeeze my eyes shut as I speak a truth that's been dancing around in the back of my mind for months now.

"May?" I ask, my voice little more than a whisper.

"Yes, my love?"

I open my eyes. "I think the best parts of my life so far have been in my daydreams."

Saying it aloud is a good kind of pain. Like working out a neglected muscle or stepping into the light after a long sleep.

She lets out a slow sigh, then slurps her tea. "Perhaps," she says lightly, refilling her teacup and adding a splash to mine as well, though I've barely touched it. "But I'm older, I'm wiser, and so I can tell you with complete confidence that there's no point with regrets. So, moving right along . . . what shall we do about it?"

The *we* makes me smile.

"Well." I pick up the teacup once more, feeling a little stronger for having aired the thought. "I guess I could use some advice on how to get out of the daydream and into real life."

"Let's start by embracing it. Your old daydream is dead—sorry, love, but it is. Bubbles is gone, and I'm going to give it to you straight: your chubby musician hasn't shown up."

"Yet," I add instinctively.

She lifts her eyebrows.

"Right. Daydreams again," I muse. "I told Caleb I'd go out with his friend. I haven't had a date in a while, so that's a start."

"It is. A good one, I'd say. Now, how about your professional life? In those daydreams you speak of, how did you spend your days?"

"Painting," I say automatically. "I paint all day, every day."

"And why is that the daydream instead of reality?"

"Well . . ." I think of Hugh Wheeler, who's still waiting on those twenty paintings, and the fierce inner debate about wanting to take advantage of the opportunity, but wanting it in my own right, not because Sebastian Andrews called in a favor.

"I've got a sabbatical, of sorts, funded by the Andrews Corporation's blood money. It's enough to tide me over until I find a new job, but I will need to find a new job."

"Painting's a job," May points out.

"Sure, if you're Botticelli living during the Renaissance. I'm trying to get *out* of the daydream, not sink further into it."

May taps her finger against her cup very gently, studying me. "What about the Chelsea art dealer?"

I look at her in surprise. I haven't told anyone about that.

She grins. "Caleb will tell you just about anything if you feed him a grilled cheese sandwich with tomato and bacon."

"Weak-willed traitor," I mutter.

"More like a loving brother. But what's the status with the art guy? Did it fall through?"

I slouch a little on the couch. "No. I haven't really pursued it."

"Really? Your brother said you were painting around the clock."

"I was. Then I found out . . ." I exhale. "The art dealer only sought me out because Sebastian Andrews told him to."

"Sebastian Andrews." She blinks. "The insanely good-looking businessman with the good butt?"

"That's him," I say grumpily, draining my tea and setting it back on the table. "Apparently, this is all part of his MO. He shuts down businesses, then tries to make himself feel better by inserting himself in his victims' lives."

I regret my words instantly. They sound petty. They *feel* untrue.

"So, just so I'm understanding the whole story," May says slowly, reaching for my saucer and beginning to fix me another perfectly sweetened cup. "A very handsome man came into your life. Offered means and opportunity to finally detach yourself from a legacy you never really wanted. Then he introduced you to someone who could turn those daydreams you're so fond of into reality. And we hate him?"

I accept the cup she hands me and stare blindly down at the tea. "Oh hell. When you put it that way, *I'm* the bad guy."

"Well, if you didn't like hearing that, you're definitely not going to like this," she says, sitting back in her chair and crossing her legs.

I look at her warily. "It gets worse?"

"You said yourself the best parts of your life are your daydreams," May says gently. "I imagine this includes your mysterious pen pal? The fantasy of what he *could* be?"

I nod.

"Would you say that the fantasy of one man is keeping you from seeing the reality of another man?"

I narrow my eyes, already knowing where she's going with this and not liking it one bit.

Or maybe . . . maybe I like it too much.

Maybe I like *him* too much.

All of a sudden, I know what comes next—what May means by embracing the uncertainty of the future.

I scowl down at my tea, then up at May. "Any chance you've got something stronger?"

She's already on the move toward the kitchen. "I thought you'd never ask."

twenty-two

Hugh Wheeler's partner is the complete opposite of the lanky, irritable art dealer. Short, round, friendly, and flamboyantly dressed, Myron Evans has gone from being a complete stranger a week ago to what feels a bit like my best friend.

I take the tissue Myron's waving at me. "Thanks. How'd you know?"

"Honey. I've witnessed lots of debut artists seeing their art displayed in a gallery for the first time. I've yet to see one who didn't cry, and that includes an impressionist who looks like Thor."

"Oh God, he was gorgeous," Hugh says, coming out from the back room, iPad in hand. "Sold well too. Shame he works so damn slow."

Myron wags a finger at his partner—a status that applies both professionally and personally—and chides him gently. "You know the rules. We never judge the artists."

"That's *your* rule," Hugh says grumpily. "Shane may be beautiful, but he is a lazy piece of shit." He looks over at me and grins. "Not like you. *You* are a delightful firecracker of a workhorse."

"Though, I notice I don't get the *gorgeous* label like the lazy impressionist," I tease.

"Your features are nicely arranged. For a female," Hugh says distractedly as he notes one of my paintings on the wall is crooked and goes to straighten it.

I look over at Myron. "I can't tell if that was a compliment or an insult."

"Always a little hard to tell," Myron said in a loud whisper.

Ignoring us, Hugh points at the painting directly in front of him. "This. It should be a series. We could do a whole jazz club."

I glance at it. It's one of my more recent works, finished in the flurry of productivity since leaving May's house a week earlier. At the center is a grand piano—white—to contrast with the woman in the red dress seated on the bench, a glass of red wine set on the side of the piano that would probably make pianists everywhere crap their pants. But it creates a moment. Behind the woman is my usual New York City backdrop—evening this time.

"I've never actually been to a jazz club," I admit.

Myron makes a dramatic gasping noise and grabs my arm, as though for balance.

"Both Myron's parents were bassists," Hugh says, and I shrug because that doesn't really mean much to me.

Myron lets out a dramatic sigh. "You don't know what a bassist is, do you?"

"Um?"

"All right, that's it. Hugh, we're taking Gracie to a jazz club."

"Agreed, mainly because I really do want this to be a set," he says, peering closer. "An old-fashioned on a stool beside the bass player. The drummer holding a Manhattan."

"With what, his third hand?" Myron asks skeptically.

"That's for Gracie to figure out," Hugh says, waving his hand. Then he turns around. "Of course, that's assuming you want to paint that. I would never presume to tell one of my artists what to work on."

Myron snorts. "Since when?"

Hugh makes a face at his partner, then turns to me, giving me a rare smile. "You should be very proud. I couldn't be more pleased."

My eyes start watering again. "Can I hug you?"

He opens his arms and makes the slightest beckoning motion with one hand.

I wrap my arms around him and squeeze him tight. "Thank you for this. You have no idea what a dream come true this is."

My daydream. My reality. A studio currently showcasing my art.

The day after I met with May, I'd gone back to work, painting with an almost feverish obsession. The paint on my twentieth work wasn't even dry when I'd texted Hugh as instructed. A day later, I'd arrived with sweaty palms and a portfolio of my best work at his Chelsea Gallery and held my breath as Myron had set each of my watercolors against the wall.

Hugh had paced back and forth, taking in every painting for what felt like an hour before turning to me and telling me he could offer me a better commission if I agreed to sell exclusively with him.

I always imagined that when my dreams came true, there'd be fireworks, champagne, and maybe some glitter.

There was none of that, of course, but the moment was still one of the best of my entire life. And yet I hadn't shared it with anyone. Mainly because the person I want to share it with hasn't been in touch since I basically ordered him out of my apartment and out of my life.

He hasn't returned my calls, and I can't blame him.

"Thanks so much for inviting me down here," I say, pushing aside the melancholy thought of never seeing Sebastian again. "I'd imagined, of course, what it would be like to see my art displayed, but actually *seeing* it . . ."

Hugh points at Myron. "His idea."

"Thank you," I say, turning to Myron, whose hot pink suit and yellow bow tie are somehow the perfect complement to Hugh's blue-and-white-striped ensemble. I hug him too.

"Thank me by learning what a bassist is," he says, patting my back. "Now, you said you had another piece to show us?"

Hugh whirls around, pushing his wire-frame glasses higher on his nose. "A new piece? Since yesterday?"

"Two, actually. I've been playing around with them for a while," I say. "They're both a bit different from my usual work. I wasn't sure if they would fit with the collection—"

"Show me." He waves at the black canvas carrying bag leaning against my calf.

I take out both pieces and set them against the blank white wall.

I bite my lip as both Hugh and Myron examine them, one the critical eye of a potential seller, the other the mostly curious examination of a man who I've quickly discovered is an over-the-top romantic like myself. I find I want both their approval, for different reasons.

Myron turns away first and draws a heart shape over the left side of his chest, mouthing *love it*. Hugh says nothing, continuing to stare at them, until he suddenly pivots on his heel. "The only thing I don't like about them is that I can't decide which I like more. They're unexpected, yes, but I think two of your best."

I exhale in relief.

"Agree," Myron says. "There's a certain longing to each of them—as though you've captured the crackle of two pivotal moments in time. What inspired them?"

I glance down at the right painting first—a woman on a pink-and-white polka-dot couch, her denim-clad legs and pink stilettos propped up on a marble coffee table. In one hand, a champagne flute. In her other, a cell phone. On her face? A secret smile, as though whatever she's looking at on her phone holds the key to her heart.

The other is a couple. A man and a woman on a park bench at night, the trees behind them shadowy. They're turned toward each other, almost reluctantly, as though pulled together by a force neither wants, and neither can resist. Adding a bit of realism to the otherwise dreamy painting is a flash of silver in each hand that any New Yorker would recognize as a spontaneous late-night snack from a food cart.

"My life," I answer quietly. "My life inspired them."

One of them inspired by my fantasy life.

The other by my *real* life.

It's time to choose.

———————

Sebastian's assistant, Noel, glances up as I step off the elevator.

"Good afternoon, Ms. Cooper. Lovely to see you again." He smiles widely, looking genuinely welcoming, which tells me Sebastian must not have confided in his assistant about the antagonistic nature of our last meeting. "How can I help you? Was something amiss with the payment check? I'd be happy to have someone from accounting—"

"No, no problems," I cut in. Then, to stall and hopefully calm my nerves, I point at the glorious bouquets flanking either side of the wide desk. "These are from Carlos and Pauline, aren't they?"

His grin widens. "Yes! You know them?"

"I do. How are they? I don't get up there as regularly anymore." I make a mental note to fix that. Just because I don't need fresh flowers for the shop doesn't mean I can't enjoy fresh flowers in my apartment.

"They're great. Considering expanding, maybe offering delivery. Some of the floors in the building liked the arrangements so much that they started ordering from them as well."

"Oh, I'm so happy for them," I say, touching a light pink rose petal.

"So, what can I help you with?"

I glance in the direction of Sebastian's closed door. "I was curious if Mr. Andrews might be available. I know I don't have an appointment, but since it's close to five, I thought I'd try my luck."

Noel studies me a moment, his curious expression turning slightly speculative.

"Sure," he says with a grin.

I blink. "Don't you need to check?"

"Hmm," he says, mostly to himself. "Better if I don't, I think. Go on in."

I give him a skeptical look, but I also know if I don't do this now, I'll chicken out.

I take a deep breath and give a quick knock.

"Yeah." Sebastian's voice is clipped, and I wince. Not a great start, and he doesn't even know it's me yet.

I step into the office and shut the door.

He doesn't look toward me right away, his attention on his computer screen as he types. His eyes cut my way, almost absently, then he stiffens.

Slowly his hands slide away from the keyboard.

"Hi," I say nervously.

He says nothing as he leans back in his chair.

I swallow, pointing back toward the door. "Noel said I could come in, but if I'm interrupting . . ."

Still nothing, but I gather my courage and walk toward him.

He looks serious and untouchable. And disinterested. Very, very disinterested.

My heart sinks.

I walk to the chair opposite his, and instead of sitting, I set my hands on the back of it, forcing myself to look into his cold aqua eyes.

"I owe you an apology," I say, my voice quiet but steady.

His eyes flash, and his fingers interlock lightly as he sets them against his mouth and watches me.

"I'm sorry for—" I laugh a little. "Well, for a lot of things. For the things I said to you. For assuming the worst about your motives. For getting angry with you for mentioning my name to Hugh, when really I should have been thanking you."

I glance down at my hands on the back of the chair. My knuckles are white. This is hard. Much harder than I realized. But I force myself to meet his eyes once more and continue.

"You're kind. I didn't want you to be. I wanted to hate you for making me see all the things that were wrong with my life. The nature of your job affects the lives of other people, and you don't take that responsibility lightly. I wanted to believe you were acting out of guilt or obligation, because it fit with my initial image of you as a heartless businessman. You aren't that. And I'm genuinely sorry."

Sebastian continues to say nothing, and my heart sinks further.

"Anyway," I say, clearing my throat awkwardly. "I just wanted you to know I don't feel good about the things I said to you, and they don't reflect how I really feel."

"Which is?"

I swallow, wondering how much to reveal. How brave to be. *I like you. I like you very much.*

But the expression on his face is so cold that I take the safe route. "I'm grateful. For the fresh start your company's afforded me. And for the chance to pursue a career in art."

Something that looks a bit like disappointment flits across

his face at my response. "I see. Well. You're welcome. And I appreciate the apology. And, for my part, I regret my high-handedness. Coming by your apartment was an invasion of privacy. Giving your information to Hugh without asking you first presumed to know too much about your . . . wants."

"But you presumed correctly. And I didn't mind you coming by my apartment."

His head snaps up, but other than that, he neither moves nor speaks. After a long moment, I force a smile that feels brittle with disappointment.

What had I expected? That he would swoop me into his arms and tell me he fell madly in love with me the moment he met me, that the other woman doesn't matter to him anymore?

"Thanks for seeing me on short notice. Have a nice evening, Mr. Andrews."

I walk back to the door, blinking back tears.

"Gracie." His voice is rough.

I turn.

He's standing, his expression both cautious and hopeful. "Do you have plans for dinner tonight?"

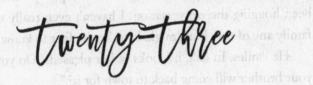

twenty-three

"That's fantastic news," Sebastian says, refilling both our glasses with the bottle of zinfandel he's ordered to go with the steaks.

I'd expected him to suggest a fancy restaurant, one of those with big glass windows and high ceilings and stuffy waiters.

Instead, he's led me to a hole-in-the-wall steakhouse with wood walls, dark lighting, and the enthusiastic buzz of people having a good time. We're seated in the back corner, enjoying delicious steaks and even more delicious mashed potatoes.

Most pleasurable of all though? The company. I can't remember the last time I've enjoyed a meal so much . . . ever.

"So, what happens now?" he asks, picking up his knife and fork, but studying me instead of cutting into his meat. "I know Hugh personally, but I don't know much about his art world."

"He wants to do a gallery opening," I say, taking a sip of water. "He hung one of my pieces already—just to generate buzz, but he's saving the rest, wants to do a whole *thing* with champagne and cocktail dresses." I laugh a little breathlessly at the sheer excitement of it all. "A gallery opening. I still can't believe it."

I sit back in my chair and smile sheepishly. "Sorry, I've been hogging the conversation. I haven't even really told my family any of this, but I'm glad you're the first to know."

He smiles. In fact, he looks rather pleased. "Do you think your brother will come back to town for it?"

"I'll invite him, definitely," I say. "But he lives in New Hampshire—about a six-hour drive—and I'd hate to have to ask him to make it twice in a month."

"The opening's happening that soon?" Sebastian says around a bite of steak.

I shrug. "Hugh said two weekends from now."

Sebastian nods, and it's on the tip of my tongue to invite him. But I hold back, knowing that if he makes some polite excuse, it'll sting, and I want to hold on to this night.

I take a bite of steak. "So, this is none of my business, but your parents were so lovely, and I keep thinking about them. How did they take the news that you and Genevieve broke up? Your mother must be disappointed."

Okay, fine. My motivations aren't *totally* pure. I know he said he and Genevieve were over for good, but it can't hurt to check . . .

He shrugs. "My mom was a bit disappointed. Genevieve is like a daughter to her though, and that doesn't change just because Gen won't be her daughter-in-law. Also, it's helped everyone that Genevieve is pregnant."

"Oh." I blink. "Wow."

Don't ask, don't ask, don't ask . . .

He smiles. "The father is an anonymous donor."

"Hmm." I take a prim little sip of wine. "Well, good for her."

"It is. She's happy. My mom's happy about getting a *sort of* second grandbaby."

"Second? You have a sibling?"

"Stepbrother," he says, picking up his wineglass. "Gary married my mom when I was seven. He has a son—Jason—from a previous marriage who lived with his mom in DC. Jason and his wife had their first baby last summer."

"Oh! I didn't realize Gary wasn't your biological father."

"He may as well have been. He adopted me. Raised me."

Something in the back of my mind flickers, telling me that this information is important somehow, but then he pours more wine, and the thought flits away.

"What's it like? Being an uncle?" I ask, scooping up the mashed potatoes. They've mixed in bits of fried onions, and it elevates the dish to a whole new level of delicious. I make a note to tell Keva about them.

"A little strange," Sebastian admits. "Jason and I are friendly, but not close. I've only met his wife once, at the wedding, and I haven't made it down to DC yet to meet Juliet. Based on the pictures she's beautiful, and fond of bows."

I smile. "Gotta love a good bow."

"You like kids?"

"I do. I certainly hope for some of my own someday," I say, thinking of Lily and the heartache of her fertility struggles. "Though lately I've made the decision to do a little less hoping and a little more acting."

He holds my gaze questioningly, and I twist my fork in the air as I chew, trying to figure out how to describe it.

"It's been brought to my attention recently," I say, setting my fork down, "by myself, that I've been living in a bit of a fantasy world."

"Fantasy as in the fairies you like to paint, or fantasy as in . . . you know." He makes a playful hubba-hubba motion with his eyebrows that seems both completely unlike him, yet somehow perfectly natural, reminding me how many layers this man seems to have.

"More like the castle-and-white-knight variety. Except the knight's a musician with tattoos and a little belly."

He blinks. "You lost me."

I find myself telling him everything. Not about Sir and him declining to want to move our relationship beyond what it is now. That's too private—too fresh. Too painful.

But I tell Sebastian all about my penchant for fairy tales. My tendency to focus on what *could* be rather than what is. My hesitancy to really, truly throw myself into the things that matter the most out of fear they won't live up to what I've built up in my mind.

"It's a real problem," I finish with a sigh.

"I don't know that it's a bad thing to know what you want," he says thoughtfully.

"No. But I'm learning it's a bad thing when you're so focused on what you *think* you want that you don't see what's right in front of you," I reply slowly.

Sebastian's fork freezes for just a fraction of a second, his fingers seeming to tighten on the utensil, his eyes flicking up to mine. The second our gazes clash, it's like that first day on the sidewalk all over again, all crackle and butterflies and Frank Sinatra.

"I know the feeling," he says quietly, still holding my gaze.

My stomach turns over on itself, and because these sort of feelings—these real-life feelings—are so very new to me I look quickly back down at my plate.

When I look up again, he's gone back to eating his steak, though there's a quiet tension between us now. Not uncomfortable. Just . . . knowing.

The server comes to clear away our plates with promises to bring the dessert menu, and Sebastian wipes his mouth, then drops the napkin into his lap, leaning forward, forearms on the table. "Can I ask you something?"

"Sure."

"Where are you at with the other guy? Mr. Complicated."

It's the one thing I wish he wouldn't have asked, and I feel a little of my lightness dim, some of my buzzy happiness fade away as I think of Sir. Of the way he *still* makes me feel.

"Actually, let me ask it another way," Sebastian says, his gaze intent. "What makes it complicated? Is he married? Is it a long-distance thing?"

I scrunch up my face and peer at him out of one squinted eye. "Promise you won't laugh?"

He nods.

"I haven't met him."

I hold my breath, waiting for the laugh, but true to his word, he doesn't. He doesn't even crack a smile.

"How'd that come about?" His voice seems different. Cautious.

Probably because he realizes he's having dinner with a lunatic.

"Oh, you know," I say, waving my hand. "The usual way. I posted naked pictures of myself online then asked if any men wanted to chat."

He rewards me with a smile, some of his tension easing. "Damn. I'm visiting the wrong websites, apparently."

I smile back, because flirtatious Sebastian is extremely likable. No. *All* parts of Sebastian are likable.

The server brings us dessert menus, and we both set the menus to the side and order coffee.

"Through a dating app," I say. "One where you get to know each other based on conversation, not appearances. The complicated bit is that I was on there for real—to meet someone. He was there quite by accident and wasn't romantically available."

The server brings over two cups and fills them with coffee, then sets sugar and cream on the table. Sebastian pushes them both toward me as though knowing exactly how I like my coffee.

"So what happened?" Sebastian asks.

I shrug. "I don't really know. He replied to my initial message, explaining his situation. I replied to that. He replied to that. Neither of us ever quit replying."

I'm braced to see amusement or judgment on his face, but instead he looks intent. "And you developed feelings for him."

I hesitate, then nod. "I know it sounds crazy. And *wrong*. He was with someone. But somehow, those messages started becoming the highlight of my day. And the way I felt when I saw his name . . . I never had those feelings in any previous relationships."

He gazes at me steadily. "You said *was* in a relationship. He's not anymore?"

I shake my head.

"Then why not meet him?"

"I tried," I say, embarrassed that my voice comes out a little cracked. "He wasn't interested. We're still friends, we still talk, but in terms of it becoming more than that . . ." I shake my head. "It's just as well. I think it's probably time to let him go. Start dating for real."

Feeling vulnerable and wanting to hide, I pick up the dessert menu and feign fascination, though the words are a little blurry and even my highly trained sweet tooth can't seem to focus or commit to anything.

I risk a look at Sebastian, and he's watching me, his knuckles drifting idly over the sharp line of his jaw as though he's lost in thought.

"What are you having?" I ask brightly. "Anything?"

He looks at me a moment longer, then slowly reaches for his menu, perusing the options as he sips his coffee. Just a splash of cream, no sugar for him.

"Want to split an ice-cream sundae?" he asks.

Grateful for the offer of normalcy after my humiliating confession, I grin. "I normally have a firm policy against splitting desserts, but based on the fact that those potatoes were more butter than vegetable, I'll make an exception."

The sundae is delicious. The conversation easy and free flowing.

Sebastian insists on paying, furthering my confusion on what this is. Does he consider me a professional associate, based on our past business? A friend?

A date?

I've got a sip of coffee left and use it as an excuse to ask one more question as he reviews the bill.

"Okay, I spilled my guts on my complicated romantic situation," I say, smiling so he won't know how much his answer matters. "What about you? How are things with Ms. Complicated? Still not the right time?"

Sebastian continues to silently study the bill for so long that I assume he's not going to answer. Finally, he scrawls his signature, closes the billfold, and looks up.

Then he surprises me by answering my question after all. "I care about her. I care about her more than she knows. I've been afraid if I tell her that, I'll lose her."

There's a fierceness in his eyes when he talks about this woman, and I look away. *Jealousy*.

Then I hear his words more clearly, and because strangely, I want to be his confidant the way he's been mine . . . "*Been* afraid," I repeat. "Past tense?"

He taps his fingers on the billfold. "I'm also not entirely sure she knows what she wants. And I want to be the *only* thing she wants."

My stomach flips at the possessive note in his tone, and jealousy strikes again. I wait for more, but he doesn't say anything.

I sigh. "That's all I'm going to get, huh? You're going to play the man-of-few-words card on this?"

"For now," he says with a smile as he stands and pulls out my chair.

The restaurant's only a fifteen-minute walk from my apartment, but Sebastian refuses to let me walk alone. And to my disappointment, he also doesn't offer to walk me. Instead he hails a cab and opens the door for me. I thank him and start to climb in, when he touches my elbow.

I freeze and look up, suddenly sandwiched between the frame of the taxi and Sebastian Andrews. Other than his fingers on my elbow he's not touching me, but he's close enough that I can feel his heat, smell his scent, see that those aqua eyes actually have a thin border of navy.

His gaze drops to my mouth for a fraction of a second, and for a heart-stopping moment, I think he might kiss me. And I know—somehow, I *know*—that it would be the kiss to ruin all other kisses.

"Your guy," he says roughly. "Do you love him?"

Considering I was just thinking about Sebastian's lips on mine, it's a jarring question.

"Everyone thinks I'm crazy to love someone I haven't met."

"That's not what I asked."

I take a deep breath, wishing I could evade the question I've been too terrified to even ask myself. But I care about him and Sir too much not to answer honestly.

"Yes," I whisper. "But it doesn't matter. It's not mutual. He won't even meet me."

Sebastian says nothing for several moments, then nods. "I think you should try again."

He pulls away and holds my gaze for a long moment before stepping back. Shaken, and confused, I climb into the cab. Sebastian waits until I pull my legs and the tail of my coat inside, then closes the door, all gentlemanly politeness.

I lean back against the cushion, barely registering that the cab smells like garlic, or that traffic is surprisingly heavy for this late in the evening. I notice only that Sebastian Andrews doesn't bother to glance at the cab as he walks away. That he's just nudged me toward another man.

And that had he asked me a second question: Is it possible to love *two* people . . .

I think I'd have had no choice but to say *yes*.

twenty-four

"So, when you said you wanted to come see my progress on the renovation, what you really meant was you wanted to . . . mope and eat my cheese?" Lily asks, wrestling the cork out of a bottle of sauvignon blanc.

"You always have the best cheese," I say around a mouthful of baguette topped with something creamy, slightly pungent, and probably very expensive.

"True, but that doesn't explain the moping."

"Not moping," I say, picking up my sister's water glass and drinking a gulp to wash down the dairy. "Thinking."

"About?"

"Boys," I say with a sigh.

"Talk," she says, pouring me a very generous glass of wine and handing it over. "For someone who's got a big gallery opening in a week, you've got puppy eyes."

"Well. I like two guys, and neither likes me back."

"Sebastian and the MysteryMate dude?" She picks up a piece of bread, carefully perusing her cheese options on the board.

"Yup."

"Well, at that girls' night, Keva and Robyn seemed pretty sure Sebastian was into you."

"Sometimes I've thought so too," I say, swirling my wine. "But we had dinner the other night. It felt almost datelike. But then at the end, he told me I should pursue the other guy."

Lily winces.

"Right?" I say glumly. "It was a pretty clear establishment of the friend zone."

"So *are* you going to pursue the other guy?"

I continue to swirl the wine. "I'm scared."

"That he's a serial killer?"

I roll my eyes. "That he'll say no again."

The second the words are out, I realize that's not what I'm *actually* afraid of.

"What if he's not who I think he is?" I ask my sister. "What if we meet, and there's zero chemistry, and we have nothing to talk about, and I'm back to being completely single, with no prospects."

What if I don't feel with him what I did that day on the side-walk with Sebastian?

Lily squeezes my knee reassuringly. "Then we'll put on some Frank, sing 'That's Life,' and keep looking."

I smile. "I like that plan."

"Me too." She pokes my knee. "I've missed this. I miss you. I'm glad we're back."

"Same. Weird though, isn't it? That shutting the doors to the store is what brought us all close again? You and I feel a little more *us*. And I've talked to Caleb more than I have in a year—did I tell you he's coming to the gallery?

"Oh God," I mutter after another thought. "Is this one more thing I have to be grateful to Sebastian Andrews for? Giving me my family back?"

She tilts her head. "You really like him, huh?"

"I do," I admit. "And maybe had things been different . . . but they're not different, so maybe . . . maybe Sebastian Andrews and I were meant to be friends?"

"Maybe," she says with a shrug. "How's that feel when you say it aloud?"

Inadequate.

I squeeze my eyes shut. "Is this my punishment for being so obsessed with Prince Charming for so long? When he finally comes along, I get two, and neither is interested?"

"Well, you don't know that your MysteryMate isn't. And actually . . ." She taps my knee again. "I've just had a thought. Maybe you don't have to give up the fairy tale, just modernize it."

I stuff the cheese wedge into my mouth. "Bigamy?"

"Funny. But no. Have you seen the new fairy tales coming out? There are still princesses and princes, but the princess isn't sitting around waiting for a dude to shove her foot into a glass slipper. The new princesses are badass. They go after what they want—"

Lily's impressive tirade is cut off by the sound of the front door opening. "Hey, Alec," I call.

"Hey, Gracie," he says, coming into the kitchen and dropping his briefcase onto the counter.

He goes immediately to Lily, setting his hands on her waist, and she grins up at him. I pause in the process of sipping my wine as I realize the tension between them over the past few months is nowhere to be seen. Instead, they look newly in love, like they can't take their eyes off each other.

"How are we?" Alec asks her softly, brushing a kiss over her lips.

"Excellent, now that you're home," she says, kissing him back. And not just a peck either.

"*Aaaaand*, that's my cue," I say, hopping down and taking one last sip of sauvignon blanc before setting it aside. "But for what it's worth, I'm really glad you guys are back."

"Me too," Lily says with a smile.

"Just curious, is there, like, a magic potion I can take to get me some of whatever fixed you two?"

"Just a good old-fashioned talk," Alec tells me, framing Lily's face with his hands. "We decided that families come in all shapes and sizes, and if ours stayed a family of two until the end, we'd count ourselves blessed to have each other."

My eyes water. *I want that.*

"Of course," Lily says playfully, "we didn't mind learning the day after that talk that we're going to be a family of three."

Her words don't register at first. And then all of a sudden they do, along with the previously missed detail that Lily poured me a glass of wine, but not one for herself.

"Wait. Oh my God. Are you pregnant?"

The twin grins on their faces answer the question, and with a happy squeal, I wrap my arms around both of them. "I'm so happy for you. Oh my God, you're going to be parents! I'm going to be an aunt! I have to learn to sew. And of course plan a Disney movie regimen. And—"

"Gracie?" Alec says, a little distracted, since he's busy kissing his wife.

"Yeah?"

"We love you. Get out," Lily answers for him.

"Okay, okay." But I sneak in one last hug before grabbing my purse and giving them their privacy.

Out on the sidewalk, I can't stop smiling as I hum "I've Got the World on a String."

Nor can I stop thinking about what Lily said about *updating* my fairy tale. No more waiting for Prince Charming.

No more waiting, period.

If I want happily-ever-after, I've got to go *get it*.

I pull out my phone and send a message.

To Sir, with a hope and a prayer,

I know we don't know what this is. I know we've been careful not to label it. Screw that. Let's find out what to label it. Let's meet. Let's give this thing a chance.

I have an art gallery opening next Saturday. I'm an artist. Have I ever told you that? There's so much I want to tell you. So much I want to know about *you*.

Please come.

Lady

My dear Lady,

I'll be there.

Yours,

Sir

Text Message from Gracie to Sebastian

Well. I did it. I asked him to meet, and he said yes. If he turns out to be a weirdo who starts out the conversation asking me what sort of saws cut through bone, this is on your head. :-)

Sebastian to Gracie

Don't overthink it. I'm sure he's something perfectly respectable. Like an aspiring magician or a mermaid aficionado.

Gracie to Sebastian

Is mermaid aficionado a real thing? Forget painting! I'm on the wrong career path . . .

Sebastian to Gracie

Not that I'm not enjoying this stint as Gracie Cooper's career coach, but how did you get my number?

Gracie to Sebastian

Myron. Told him we're friends but that I'd accidentally deleted your number from my phone.

Sebastian to Gracie

Are we? Friends?

Gracie to Sebastian

Depends. Will you come to my art opening?

Sebastian to Gracie

I want nothing more, but I have something going on that night.

Gracie to Sebastian

Ah. Finally decide to make it the Right Moment with Ms. Complicated?

Sebastian to Gracie
Actually, yes. Wish me luck that I'm not too late.

Gracie to Sebastian
Ooooh, sorry. I'm going to be needing all the luck in the universe that night to make sure that my guy doesn't have any weird collections or fetishes.

Sebastian to Gracie
Some friend you are. But you're right, you DO need all the luck. At least I know what Ms. Complicated looks like. YOUR guy could be super into face paint.

Gracie to Sebastian
With that kind of attitude, you're never going to get an invitation to the wedding.

Sebastian to Gracie
Wedding? You move fast.

Gracie to Sebastian
Cinderella knew in one night.

Sebastian to Gracie
Cinderella also wore shoes made of glass.

Gracie to Sebastian
Good idea! I've got just the dress to pair them with.

Sebastian to Gracie
Are you nervous?

Gracie to Sebastian
About cutting up my feet? A little.

Sebastian to Gracie
Gracie.

Gracie to Sebastian
Heck yes, I'm nervous. I've been so worried about him not living up to my expectations that I'm only now starting to realize something far worse: What if I don't live up to HIS?

Sebastian to Gracie
Impossible.

Sebastian to Gracie
. . . But in case he seems less than enthralled, you could always cook for him. I've heard you make a mean crab cake.

Gracie to Sebastian
Hilarious. I think I liked you better when we were enemies.

Sebastian to Gracie
Ah-ha! But you admit that you DO like me . . .

twenty-five

"Okay, I think the fact that Mystery Man signed it Yours means something," Keva says, handing my phone back and rummaging in her makeup bag. "That's the first time he's signed it that way?"

"No, he always signs it Yours, but it's usually sort of playful. Like Yours *in* something relevant to the conversation . . . ice cream, understanding, constipation—"

"I'm sure he's never signed it yours in constipation," a male voice interjects from across the room. "If he has, you should seriously reconsider this meeting."

"You said if you were going to stay, you wouldn't interrupt girl talk," I tell Sebastian with a scowl from my kitchen table where Keva is putting finishing touches on my makeup for the gallery opening in an hour.

"No, *you* said I couldn't interrupt girl talk. I never agreed," Sebastian says with a grin.

"Remind me again what he's doing here?" Keva asks, using the eyeliner to gesture over her shoulder at Sebastian.

"I brought her congratulatory flowers since I can't go to her big night," Sebastian says, pointing at the gorgeous assortment of pink blooms. "We're friends now."

"A status I'll have to revoke if you keep eating my emergency stash of chocolate chips," I tell him.

Keva taps her eyeliner on her palm. "Sebastian, you're a dude. What do you think this guy meant with the *Yours*. That is some intimate shit, right?"

"Sure," he says, taking a sip of water.

"I'm still iffy on this plan," Keva says. "I'm all for bold moves, but if he's a real weirdo, that could put a major damper on the evening. Don't worry though, Grady agreed to keep an eye out tonight."

"Oh, is *that* why Grady's your plus one?" I tease gently.

"Hush, unless you want to leave this chair looking like an eighties workout instructor," Keva replies. But she's smiling a little, and it's the glowing, secret smile of a woman about to spend the evening with a man she's been into for a long time.

"I hope Mystery Man's got a gap between his teeth," Keva says. "I've got a lot riding on this."

"*You* have a lot riding on it?" I ask incredulously. "What about me?"

"Fair enough. I meant *financially* I have a lot riding on this."

I narrow my eyes, and she gives me a guilty grin. "There may or may not be a wager."

"*What?*"

"Most popular theory so far is that he's middle-aged and lonely, though there's some debate on whether he'll have fake hair or a comb-over."

"A toupee could be nice," Sebastian says.

I glare at him, then turn back to Keva.

"Who's in on the wager?" I demand.

"Pretty much everyone," Keva says with a grin. "It was my idea." She bows. "But your sister, her husband. Robyn, May, Rachel, your brother, even Josh, though that little sweetie thinks your guy's big secret is that he's a vegan Navy SEAL."

Sebastian snorts.

"All right, all right, all right," I say, nodding thoughtfully. "I can be a good sport about this, but I want in on the wager."

"Ooh, twist!" Keva says in delight. "Hold on, let me pull up the spreadsheet."

"There's a spreadsheet?" I lift up my hands. "Nope, that's fine. Love it. Okay, so I already know who he is."

Sebastian's been idly inspecting the paintbrushes I've set in a cup on my counter to dry, but he looks up abruptly. "You do?"

"Yup," I say confidently. "Well, no. But I know exactly what he looks like."

"I'm ready. Shoot," Keva says.

I give her a look. "You already know this."

"Right, right, *the* guy," she says, her thumbs already working.

"What guy?" Sebastian asks.

"Her dream guy," Keva explains, turning toward him, fingers still flying over her iPhone. "Long brown hair, not too tall, not too fit. Musician."

"Lives in Brooklyn. Maybe Alphabet City," I say. "I'm unclear on that. But his smile's perfectly imperfect. That, I'm definitely clear on. He's got a tiny chip from a baseball incident—"

"He's a musician *and* plays baseball?" Sebastian asks.

"It's her fantasy. Don't take this away from her," Keva says with a smile.

For the first time since he's shown up, a shadow cuts through Sebastian's cocky playfulness, and he looks almost vulnerable.

Then he straightens up and extends a hand for Keva's phone. "My turn."

"For what?" I demand, even as Keva hands him her cell without hesitation.

"I want in on the wager," he says.

I roll my eyes and obediently pucker so Keva can apply a glittery light pink gloss, then adds something sparkly to my cheeks and brow bones.

"Perfect," Keva says, stepping back and surveying my face. "Damn, I'm good. Bastian, look at my genius."

Sebastian looks up, momentarily startled at the nickname, then glances over at me. His mouth tilts in the corner. "She looks a bit like . . ."

"Sexy Tinker Bell," Keva says. "All those glittery, whimsical paintings of hers come to life."

"They're not *all* glittery and whimsical," I mutter, reaching for a hand mirror. "Oh. *Oh*."

"See?" Keva says, a little bit smug.

"It's perfect," I admit. She's added just the right amount of shimmer so I don't look like a preteen movie princess, but sort of like a fairy, a sexy fairy, with all the dark smudging she added beneath my eyes.

Sebastian hands Keva her phone back, and she glances

down at what he's entered before giving him a speculative look. "Interesting. Very interesting."

"What?" I say, extending my palm. "Let me see."

Sebastian opens his mouth, but Keva's already shaking her head and tucking her phone into her back pocket. "Nope. We'll see who won the wager at the end of the evening, and for now, I want *you*"—she points at me—"to focus on getting dressed. And I— Holy moly, is that the time? I need to go get myself fancy."

She gathers the rest of her makeup and tucks it under her arm. "We still taking a car together?" she asks. "They're not like sending you a limo or something?"

I laugh. "I don't think I'm quite to limo level yet."

"Soon though," Keva says, wagging a finger. "Very soon you're going to take the art world by storm, and I'll be making food for all the celebrities paying thousands for a ticket to fight for the chance to buy your pieces."

"I'd be happy if a noncelebrity bought *one* of my pieces," I say, letting the nerves I've been battling all day slip out.

Keva rolls her head over to Sebastian. "Bastian, I'm assigning you pep talk duty. I've got to get ready."

"On it," he says.

"Perfect," Keva says. "Gracie, see you in—crap, twenty-two minutes?" My front door slams, and I hear thuds as Keva takes the stairs two at a time.

"I don't need a pep talk," I tell him.

"You sure?" he asks.

No. I pick up the vase of flowers he brought me and inhale.

"Every piece will sell," Sebastian says with quiet confidence.

I look up in surprise. "You can't know that."

He smiles innocently. "As you know, I have excellent business sense."

"You know what *fails*. I've yet to see your chops when it comes to sensing when something will succeed."

"Ah, but the *More* part of your store didn't fail," he says lightly. "The fact that tonight is happening is proof that while there may not be a market for a niche champagne shop in Midtown, there is a market for Gracie Cooper paintings."

"I'd never thought of it that way," I say. "Thank you."

"You're welcome." Our gazes hold for a moment, and I forget that I'm supposed to have moved him to the friend column.

That he has someone else, and that as of tonight, I might too.

He straightens and steps nearer so I have to tilt my head up to meet his eyes. "I wish you could be there," I whisper before I can stop myself.

Sebastian reaches for my hand and squeezes. "It'll work out the way that it should. Trust me."

His hand drops, and he steps back and turns away. I bite back a protest. This feels *wrong*.

"Sebastian." He turns back around, his eyes bright with something I don't recognize.

"Why?" I ask softly. "*Why* did you tell me to pursue the other guy?"

He steps closer, lifting a hand to rest his fingertips lightly against my cheek. "Because you said you loved him. Because you deserve your fairy-tale ending. And because I'd do anything for you, Gracie Cooper. Even if it means letting you go."

twenty-six

I don't have time to dwell, and maybe that's a good thing—I'm afraid I would cry and never stop. Or abort the whole evening altogether out of sheer overwhelming panic. But somehow I manage a smile and let Keva distract me on the way to the studio.

From then on, it's been a blur.

May cries when she sees me, then proceeds to take about a hundred photos. Myron comes over and starts to tell her there's no photography in the gallery but backs off when she compliments his velvet boots. Or maybe because her earrings tonight are a grenade and a machete. In case *your guy is a dud and needs to be taught a lesson*.

"May," Lily says in laughing exasperation as May motions for Caleb, Lily, and me to stand side by side. Again. "What are you going to do with these pictures?"

"Take them to Heaven to show your mom and dad," May says in all seriousness, clearly irked that she even has to explain this.

"I don't know what's more ballsy," Caleb says out of the corner of his mouth as he puts his arm around my shoulder.

Lily's arm slips around my waist from the other side. "That she thinks Heaven allows cell phones or that she thinks she's going there."

"You mind your tongue, Caleb Cooper," May says as she snaps the photo. "Or I'll be telling your lady friend here all about the way you once had to ask your dad why your underwear had an open flap in the front and your sisters' didn't."

"You weren't even there for that!" Caleb says as Michelle, his girlfriend, laughs beside May.

"Yes, but your father was, and you never forget a story like that." May looks down at her phone and, finally satisfied, drops it into her shark-shaped clutch.

"He was fourteen," I whisper loudly.

He swats the back of my head.

Alec appears carrying an impressive amount of champagne flutes, which he hands around.

Lily takes the *tiniest* sip of Alec's since she can't have her own. "Ooh. That's excellent!"

"Of course it is, I picked it," Robyn says, appearing from nowhere with a wide grin, dressed to kill in a red dress that matches the lipstick Keva bought for her.

"Well done," May says, clinking her glass to Robyn's, all smiles for her now that they no longer have to work together and bicker over how long May's sushi lunch break went. "It's delicious."

"Quick toast to our lady of the night," Alec says.

"Well, that makes her sound like a prostitute, but sure," Lily says, earning what I'm pretty sure is a quick pinch on the butt from her husband. She giggles. Actually *giggles*, and it's the best thing I've heard in forever. It's like a front-row seat to happily ever *after* after.

"To Gracie," Alec continues, his arm around Lily's waist as he smiles at me.

We all lift our glasses, and my eyes water a little at the near perfection of the moment.

"You're a hit," Rachel says, coming up behind me. "I've been doing regular laps of the room, and the Sold signs are going up like crazy."

"My personal favorite painting was sold before we even got here," Lily says with a little pout.

"Which one?" I ask in surprise. From the moment I'd arrived, Myron and Hugh swept me into a flurry of introductions and who's who and heaps of praise, the latter of which had made me feel like flying, even as I try not to think about the one person who won't be here—and the one person who will.

"I just love the one of the couple in Central Park at night. I don't know what it is, but it gave me goose bumps," my sister is saying, giving a little shiver. "It's so romantic."

"*My* favorite is the one of the woman on her phone," Michelle says. "Am I right in thinking that's the only self-portrait of the bunch?"

"Yes, actually," I say, surprised but not displeased that Caleb's lovely new girlfriend is so astute. "I mean, it's stylized. My legs aren't that long, I never wear heels, the hair's a bit too glamorous, but yeah. Me!"

"That one also sold before we got here," Alec says.

"*Really?*" I say, genuinely surprised. Not because I don't

think they're good—they're my favorites—but because they're less flashy than the rest.

Lily shrugs. "Hugh—or Myron, I didn't catch who was who during the flurry of introductions—said one of their regulars came by earlier today and offered *twice* the asking price. They accepted, hoping it would give a sense of urgency to the other potential buyers."

"Well, it worked," Rachel says gleefully. "You're never going to be able to keep up with the demand now, Gracie."

"Of course she will," May says. "But we'll figure all that out later. I think what we all want to know is why is *he* a no-show."

All of my friends' and family's eyes swing toward me, plainly curious, and I smile even though my heart feels like it's beating a million miles an hour in anticipation. "Not a no-show," I explain. "I told him to arrive an hour after this whole thing started. I wanted to make sure I had plenty of time to meet everyone Hugh wanted me to. And to spend time with you guys."

"Okay, we've got—" Lily tilts Alec's wrist toward her so she can see the time. "Well, any minute now."

My stomach flips, and it takes all my self-control not to turn and stare at the front door until he comes through it.

"Or, he could already be here, mingling among us, planning his move," Caleb says, rubbing his hands together and peering at the crowd, which has gotten noisier and noisier as the champagne's been flowing.

"He's not."

"Well, respectfully, babe, you wouldn't know," Rachel points out.

"We agreed on a visual cue. He knows I'll be wearing a pink-and-white dress—"

"Which is stunning on you, by the way."

"Thank you," I say, smiling at Caleb's girlfriend, who's obviously looking for brownie points with the family, but I don't mind it in the least. "And he will have . . . well I'm not going to tell you; you'll think it's corny."

"Probably," Caleb confirms as I continue to scan the room for the agreed-upon signal.

Me in a pink-and-white dress, him with a single pink rose in his suit pocket.

It had been Sir's idea, and at the time it had seemed like a good one—romantic. But now, pink flowers make me think of the bouquet sitting on my kitchen table, which makes me think of Sebastian . . .

"Oh, excuse me," I say in apology to my group as I see Hugh pointedly waving me over to where he is speaking with a white-haired man.

"Gracie, this is Doug Frey," Hugh says. "One of our most enthusiastic patrons."

The older man shakes my hand with a firm grip and friendly smile. "I was just asking Hugh here if I might be able to commission something like this."

He points, and I turn to the Central Park–bench painting Lily had taken a fancy to. The one that was so quick to sell.

"My grandson proposed to his girl on a bench in Central Park a few weeks ago. I wasn't there, obviously, but they had a friend take a photo, and it wasn't too unlike this, though he was on one knee."

Hugh's eyes are wide, and he's nodding dramatically behind Mr. Frey's shoulder indicating that I'd be an idiot to say no.

"Of course," I say, smiling at the older gentleman. "I'd love to hear more about what you're looking for. Perhaps we can discuss it next week?"

"Hugh has my info. Though, damn—you're sure I can't sweet-talk you into giving me the name of whoever snatched this one up before I saw it?" he asks, turning to Hugh with a mischievous smile. "The colors would look fantastic in my living room, and the foil wrappers remind me of lunches when I was a paralegal in my twenties over on Fifth and Sixty-Third . . ."

"Sorry," Hugh says, not looking even remotely sorry. "The buyer of this one seemed quite set on it. I can't imagine him wanting to sell."

"Me neither."

I whirl around at the familiar voice, though it's one I hadn't expected to hear tonight, no matter how desperately I wanted to.

I find myself grinning into his smiling aqua eyes, and acting purely on instinct, I fling my arms around his neck. "You decided to come!"

He hugs me back, strong and sure, and when I start to pull away, his arms tighten almost imperceptibly as though hesitant to let me go. He releases me and turns to Mr. Frey.

"Doug, good to see you again. It's been a while."

The older man smiles and shakes Sebastian's hand. "You're not usually so quick on the draw with Hugh's pieces, but I should have known you'd get the drop on me one of these days."

"I'm not usually so quick on the draw with *Hugh's* pieces, no," Sebastian clarifies. "But with Gracie Cooper originals, on the other hand, it took some restraint to limit myself to these two."

It takes me a second to register the meaning of his words, and I look up. "Wait. *You* bought these? Why?"

Sebastian's eyes are warm as they look down at me. "I should think it would be obvious." His voice is quiet, meant for my ears only, and as though sensing they're no longer a part of the conversation, Hugh and Doug Frey tactfully shift away to mingle with the rest of the guests.

I feel flustered. And confused. And anticipatory, like I'm on the edge of something life changing but missing a key piece of the puzzle.

"The Central Park one, I guess I understand," I say. "But the other, that's—"

"You and your mystery man," Sebastian finishes for me before glancing around the room curiously. "Speaking of, where is he?"

Horrified to realize I'd forgotten about the big meeting after Sebastian's surprise arrival, I quickly scan the men in the room. There are plenty of suits. No pink roses. My heart sinks, but I remind myself he could simply be running late, or gathering his courage . . .

"He'll be here," I say stubbornly, still peering through the crowd, because I need to believe it. Because every part of my heart believes that this is my night, that this is my man, that—

"Gracie." Sebastian says my name quietly, the ache of it wrapping around my heart and pulling me back around to face him.

I meet his eyes, and the tender expression makes me furious with frustration and longing. How dare he do this now, how dare he make me wish—

A flash of pink catches my eye.

I drop my gaze to his chest. To his suit pocket, where a single perfect pink rose is tucked, a simple, sweet beacon calling me home.

My mind whirls, and I shake my head in confused denial at the flower. "How did you—I didn't tell—the only person who knew about the pink rose . . ."

Oh my God.

There's only one way Sebastian Andrews could know what to wear tonight. Only one reason he'd want *both* paintings, the one of him and me and . . .

The *other* one of him and me. Of me and Sir.

Because they're one and the same.

My eyes close as all the pieces slowly fit together. The overlaps between the two men. The revelation that Gary isn't Sebastian's biological dad, which means that Sebastian's real father could be dead . . . just like Sir's.

The pink flowers today, a hint, a promise. The other woman, the complicated one he couldn't bear to lose. *Me.*

I open my eyes and slowly lift my gaze to his, where he seems to be holding his breath, his heart and hope in his eyes.

"It's you," I say softly. "It's always been you."

"Yes." He whispers it, his hand lifting toward my face, hesitating. Then, very gently, he sets his fingers to my cheek, his thumb catching a tear I didn't realize had fallen. "*Yes*."

"When did you know?" I ask as his fingers trace over my cheek tenderly.

"Your cat's name was the first jolt. That Gracie's and Lady's cats were both named Cannoli caught me off guard. Then you passionately defended gelato, which was familiar. After that, I went back and read every message, and I could only hear your voice. Then that night at dinner, you told me all about—"

"*You*," I say with a smile. "I told you all about yourself."

"You told me about *us*." He smiles back, the palm on my cheek more sure now, his eyes warm as they touch on my every feature, as we see each other finally, as we fully are. His gaze drops to my mouth, his head lowers.

"Wait." I put a hand to his chest, lightly. "Why not tell me at dinner? Why this whole thing?"

"Well, because I was ninety-nine percent sure, but since my heart was on the line as well, I wanted that last one percent. And I knew that if Lady asked Sir to the art show, I'd have it. And because . . ." That same flicker of vulnerability I've seen before, the one that tugs deep at my heart flits across his face, and he glances down, embarrassed. "I'm not the easiest guy to love. Not by a long shot, and I wanted—" He takes a deep breath. "I wanted you to love *both* Sebastian and Sir. Because I'm a selfish ass, and I wanted you to love both sides of me, as much as I love both sides of you. And because of what I said before—you deserve the fairy-tale ending, and I can only hope you'll give me a chance to be *yours*, Gracie."

I wipe my eyes impatiently, since the tears are blurring my vision, and now that I've found him, I don't want to miss a second of looking at his face. "I should hate you. Do you have *any* idea how it tore me up? I was so sure Sir was my soul mate, but then *Sebastian* showed up, and I couldn't stop thinking about him. And then I was falling in *love* with both—"

His mouth closes over mine, our lips fitting together perfectly, and his hand slowly slides around my waist, his palm spreading wide on my back and pulling me closer.

It's a fairy-tale kiss.

Okay, fine, it's a PG-13 fairy-tale kiss, with tongues and hands, and a lot of cheering and whoops from the crowd.

Someone yells, "Get a room!" Caleb.

Someone blows their nose loudly. May.

Wolf whistle. Keva. Or maybe Rachel.

Cheering mixed with the occasional sob. Lily.

And then something warm and invisible seems to wrap around us. Squeezing. Loving.

Dad. Mine. His. My mom.

Sebastian pulls back slowly, his thumb reverently touching my bottom lip, and he smiles down at me, looking every bit as happy as I feel.

"You know," I say teasingly, touching a finger to the pink rose. "If you want to snatch up all my paintings of us, you should have made it a trio. The one of the guy in the suit and the aqua eyes? That's you."

"I know," he says with a mischievous grin. "I knew the second I saw it in your living room."

"But you didn't want it? You didn't like it?"

"I like it. I like it a lot, and I *really* like knowing that you were thinking about me as often as I was thinking about you."

"But . . . ?"

He lowers his head to whisper playfully. "But I'll be honest, I thought it would be a little vain to have a painting of myself hanging in our home."

I let out a stunned laugh. "*Our* home? Getting a little ahead of yourself, aren't you there, Sir?"

"My dear Lady, you stole my heart twice. If you think I'm letting another second of my life pass without you in it, I'll have to kiss you again to set you straight."

And he does.

Cinderella's glass slipper? It's got nothing on Sebastian Andrews's kiss.

Epilogue

One Year Later

To Sir, with suspicion,

As an anniversary gift, Keva sent me the spreadsheet with the wagers you all made that night of my show at the gallery.

You described yourself *exactly*. Seeing as you had an unfair advantage, you, *sir*, should forfeit your prize.

Lady

_____

My dear Lady,

I'll gladly return the hundred bucks, but I'm not giving back the prize: you.

Yours in victory,

Sir

_____

To Sir, with begrudging respect,

Well played. Also, did you get the anniversary gift I sent to your office? I call it *Man with the Aqua Eyes, the Sequel.*

Lady

_____

My dear Lady,

I did. You might have mentioned that it was a nude.

My mother saw it.

Yours in *I will never recover,*

Sir

_____

To Sir, with glee,

Be grateful. Hugh and Myron insisted that if I agreed to display it in the gallery, it'd fetch my highest sale price yet.

Lady

My dear Lady,

I'm ignoring that. Did you get *my* anniversary gift?

Yours in wondering,

Sir

To Sir, with love,

A bassinet shaped like Cinderella's slipper for Baby Girl Andrews? I'm still trying to find the words.

Lady

Gracie,

Find them later. Quit texting me from the living room and come to bed.

Your loving husband,

Sebastian

Author's Note

Dear Reader,

Thank you so much for reading *To Sir, with Love*. If you've made it this far, I hope that means you finished the book, and I hope even more that you enjoyed reading it as much as I enjoyed writing it.

Sebastian and Gracie's story is one that's been with me for years—long before I typed the words *Chapter One*. Nora Ephron is one of my heroes, and *You've Got Mail* has always been my favorite of her works. But as strongly as I felt called to tell my own version of a couple who fell in love *twice*—once in person and once over "letters"—it took me a good long while to figure out what *my* version of that love story looked like.

In the 1937 Hungarian play *Parfumerie* by Miklós László (the original!), it was letters. In 1940's *The Shop Around the Corner*, as well as in the musicals *In the Good Old Summertime* and *She Loves Me*, it was also letters.

In 1998, Nora Ephron updated the story in *You've Got Mail* to business rivals falling in love over email. In *To Sir, with Love*, I wanted to bring that wonderful, classic premise into the twenty-first century, and being a millennial (albeit an *elder* millennial), for me that meant Gracie and the mysterious Sir falling in love over, what else: an app.

One thing that struck me, even as I wrote Gracie constantly checking her phone in a very twenty-first-century kind of way, is the *timelessness* of this story. Gracie breathlessly waiting for a notification on her app didn't feel so different from Margaret Sullavan and James Stewart checking their physical mailboxes in *The Shop Around the Corner* in 1940. Or Meg Ryan and Tom Hanks listening to that unmistakable '90s sound (to those of us who remember it) of AOL connecting to the Internet, holding their breath in the hopes that they'd hear those three little words: *You've got mail!*

I realized that while I set out to create a modern homage to *Parfumerie*, in the end, it didn't matter whether it was a letter, an email, a postcard, a telegram, a text, or a message in a dating app. This is not a story about technology or the specific means of communication. This is a story about hope. It's about determined optimism that the person on the other side of that written communication *will* be every bit as wonderful as he or she seems to be. It's a story about the folly of first impressions, about forgiveness and growth, about kindness and friendship.

Handwritten letters may be increasingly becoming a thing of the past, but those feelings of finding yourself and falling in love never go out of style. It's my fondest hope that I've captured those feelings in these pages.

The early stages of this story happened inside my head—years' worth of musing, of discovering the characters, of uncovering the story's essence, and *lots* of early mornings hunched over my laptop at 5 a.m., desperately trying to type the story as quickly as it was unfolding in my imagination.

Upon finishing the first draft, however, *To Sir, with Love* became a group effort, in the best sort of way. This story absolutely would not exist in its current form without the hard work, patience, and genius of my editor, Sara Quaranta. She seemed to know what I was trying to do with the story better than I did, and somewhere amidst the pesky world of revisions, I uncovered not only the heart of the story but also a new friend in Sara.

I am so fortunate to have discovered an incredible publishing partner in Gallery. Their support for me, and this book, has been almost palpable. A huge thank-you to Lisa Litwack and Connie Gabbert for understanding so thoroughly the cover this story needed, even before it was finished. To Faren Bachelis and Crissie Johnson Molina, for their enviable attention to detail as they patiently polished all my writing's rough edges. And especially to Christine Masters, who I'm convinced is some sort of wizard, with the magical ability to take tens of thousands of words and whip them into book-shape.

And, as always, no Lauren Layne book would exist in the world without the unwavering support of Nicole Resciniti, my amazing agent, whose belief in me has never wavered since those early days when she plucked my messy first manuscript out of the slush pile and gave me a shot at making my dreams come true.

I also need to thank my inner circle—the people who know me not as Lauren Layne, but simply as Lo, or Fern, or "Well, Lauren always did read a lot as a kid, so I guess it makes sense she's turned into a hermit writer now . . ." Your love and support, even while I disappear for weeks at a time inside a manuscript, mean the world to me. To my husband, Anthony, in particular, for refilling my coffee cup without my asking, for making me meals even when I'm deep into a scene and probably forget to say thank you. I love my book heroes, but make no mistake: *you* are the real hero.

To all of my readers, especially those who've been with me since my earliest Stiletto days, who patiently go along with whatever my Muse feels like writing, who offer words of encouragement and who I feel—truly feel—silently cheering me on, even when I take a step back from social media and "public life" to focus on my writing. I'm very grateful for you, and I appreciate you, even when I'm quiet. Especially when I'm quiet.

And lastly, to Miklós László for creating a story so wonderful, so beloved that it's inspired writers and creators many times over, and to the late, great Nora Ephron for being so freaking fabulous.

xo.

Lauren Layne

December 2020